THENNBERG

or

SEEKING TO GO HOME AGAIN

Studies in Austrian Literature, Culture, and Thought

Translation Series

György Sebestyén

THENNBERG

OR

SEEKING TO GO HOME AGAIN

Translated by Lisa Fleisher

Afterword by Michael Mitchell

ARIADNE PRESS

Ariadne Press would like to express its appreciation to the Austrian Cultural Institute, New York and the Austrian Ministry of Education, Vienna for their assistance in publishing this book.

Translated from the German *Thennberg oder Versuch einer Heimkehr*, ©1969 Verlag Kurt Desch, Munich

Library of Congress Cataloging-in-Publication Data

Sebestyén, György.
   [Thennberg, oder, Versuch einer Heimkehr. English]
   Thennberg, or, Seeking to go home again / György Sebestyén: translated by Lisa Fleisher; afterword by Michael Mitchell.
     p.   cm. -- (Studies in Austrian literature, culture, and thought. Translation series)
   ISBN 0-929497-84-8
   I. Title. II. Title: Thennberg. III. Title: Seeking to go home again. IV. Series.
   PT2681.E2T4713   1995
   833'.914--dc20   93-33731
                                                      CIP

Cover design:
Art Director: George McGinnis
Illustrator: David Prock

Copyright ©1995
by Ariadne Press
270 Goins Court
Riverside, CA 92507

All rights reserved.
No part of this publication may be reproduced or transmitted in any form or by any means without formal permission.
Printed in the United States of America.
ISBN 0-929497-84-8

György Sebestyén

If you haven't got anything to eat, Markus Löw had said to him, go find a brook and catch a fish. Finding a brook is no big deal, you can find a brook anywhere, some brook or other, and where there's a brook there's a fish too, you catch it with a basket or with an empty tin can or with your hand, you grab him by the tail and bang his head against a rock. You can find a rock anywhere, some rock or other, and after that you make a fire and you take the gut out of the fish and you put a twig in his mouth, and then you grill the fish and still your hunger. That's how he said it, still your hunger. And then he went on, without good-bye, without a handshake, without turning his head, went on, past the body of crazy Adalbert Friedländer and toward the barrack, where for the last months they had lain side by side, close together when it was cold, on a sack of straw that hadn't had any straw in it for a long time, under a horse blanket that hadn't been a blanket for a long time but that was a gray rag, stiff with dirt around the edges, the rest like a ragged sieve.

So on to Thennberg, maybe I'll come by, Markus Löw had said then, and after that he went on, without good-bye, although he was a polite man, too polite even, ridiculously polite. Strobl, for instance, every time he met him, he would greet him with a little bow, my compliments, Herr Strobl, he would say every time, the way he probably used to say to his customers, or to the handful of Jews in his little hometown in front of the prayer house on a Saturday morning. My compliments, Herr Strobl, he would say with a smile, even though none of that would have been necessary anymore in the last days, because SS-man Strobl—a baker's apprentice from Ottakring in civilian life, so they said—had first discarded the energetic nordic German he had used to give his commands, and then the facial expression of a hellish fiend which he obviously really wasn't, and finally he had nothing left except his dog, but now he led him on a leash. The rest of the fiends who had guarded the concentration camp until now had evaporated, because the Russians were going to arrive any moment, within three days at the latest, only Strobl had stayed. Maybe he had secret connections with the Russians, maybe he was waiting for new orders, maybe he had gone crazy like Adalbert Friedländer, who could tell?

Anyway, he was here, and at six o'clock sharp in the morning and at twelve o'clock sharp at noon and at six o'clock sharp in the evening he took his dog for a walk. Some wanted to string him up together with his dog, and others looked past him because they didn't have the strength left to do anything else but look past everybody and everything, but Markus Löw continued to greet him politely, he bowed gently, which looked like a scarecrow flapping in the wind, he said, my compliments, Herr Strobl, no doubt he wanted it to come out loud and clear and he couldn't help it if it came out weak and squeaky as if each word were a rusty pail on a rusty chain that you had to pull out of a dirty well with the help of a winch in need of lubrication. And then he smiled. It looked funny, that smile: in the face of Markus Löw, white and like plaster under the stubble, suddenly a dark hole would appear, and at the same time the head would drop slightly to the right. One time Adalbert Friedländer was standing there too, and after Strobl had passed by he said the following: You look as if someone had stepped on your face, just like a clown. Strobl pretended to be busy with his dog or with distant events not visible to others, every time Markus Löw greeted him he did that; but then, when the Russians had actually arrived and led Strobl away, he didn't bend down to his dog anymore because the dog had been shot by a uniformed Russian boy, instead he looked past Markus Löw and the others into the distance, and of all things at that lonely tree on which they had wanted to string him up, those who were so furious.

If you haven't got anything to eat, Markus Löw began, but he didn't say more because just then crazy Friedländer was being brought out of the barrack, Friedländer, a second-hand dealer who had remained physically healthy, even strong, stronger than any of the others, and who perhaps for this reason hadn't been taken to one of the extermination camps with the rest of the crazies, the deathly ill, the weakened, the obstreperous, and the ones who just had bad luck. Even before the arrival of the Russians he had disappeared into the now empty guard barrack and had made separate piles of any blankets that had been left behind, any discarded uniform jackets, worthless boots, ripped-off badges of rank, providing himself with a new outfit in the process. Strobl had watched him, without saying a word, maybe he did say something, there was really no way of knowing, the fact is that Adalbert Friedländer barricaded himself in the barrack, and when the Russians entered the barrack he squatted behind his rags, behind his newly acquired stock and in his newly acquired uniform, and from there pelted the soldiers with the shabbiest shoes, useless as merchandise, with empty bottles and with chairs. Then he stood in front of the barrack. They tied his hands together in back. He screamed. The rosy-cheeked youth who had shot Strobl's dog touched Friedländer's chest with the muzzle of his machine pistol, and then stepped aside to avoid the horizontally squirting stream of blood. At the same moment a truck drove up, loaded with bread and lard; one could hardly hear the shot.

So anyway, the brook and the fish and the rock, and you still your hunger, Markus Löw had said to him and had gone back to the barrack past Friedländer's body, without good-bye, that may have been yesterday, maybe the day before, and now there were trees on both sides of the road that led to Thennberg (by a detour perhaps but anyway to Thennberg), trees made out of stillness, grown in stillness, still trees, grown stillness, the words rolled around in his head, this way and that, hollow ones and solid ones, solid at first and then again hollow, words like soap bubbles and words like balls of lead; sparse woods lay on either side of the road which was already free of snow. Water had collected in the ruts, first from melted snow and water from the spring rains after that; out of clouds that had blown in from distant lands; everything was distant; the chronological sequence in his memory had collapsed, like a house of cards at a single, gentle touch. He didn't know, for instance, with absolute certainty whether Strobl had led his dog on a chain or on a leash, or whether Adalbert Friedländer had gone crazy only just before the Russians came or earlier, he couldn't remember the color of Markus Löw's eyes, it seemed to him that Markus Löw had dark eyes the whole time, but on the last day they had suddenly been gray, gray-blue and lifeless, eyes of stone. And what about the road that led to Thennberg: did it really lead to Thennberg? There had been a well at one time, a rusty bucket had dangled from a rusty chain, and the wheel had been squeaky, and that squeaking had sounded like the hoarse, long yowling of the cats who at night sat on the roof-top or somewhere in one of the plane-trees, cats in the moonlight, he had not seen any since he was fourteen, and after that, for six years, he had not been aware of moonlight, not as moonlight but merely as gloomy, washed-out light that sometimes made the nights dangerous, that made the barbed wire glitter and the train tracks and the tops of boots and the bald heads, a malignant light, icy even in summer, life-threatening. Twenty-two minus five makes seventeen, at seventeen he had been taken to the concentration camp, the first one, and fourteen he had been, not quite fourteen, that last summer vacation in Thennberg; that too was a game, that counting, like the words, the years were solid one time, hollow the next.

To play, just to play, with words and with memories and with the rhythm of the steps. Memory was a damp basket in which lay a large piece of sweetish-smelling meat. It felt heavy, as if it lay on the stomach. The stomach bulged out, like a hemisphere; The Russians had distributed bread and lard, along with that came sharp, tongue-corroding brandy that heaved up the half-chewed, just gulped-down stuff. You filled up, then you vomited, then you filled up again, it killed some, they lay there like the dying, after the undigested mass came gushing out bloody from their mouth and from their anus; some survived, they cowered in a corner, didn't eat the lard since it came from pig and the Law is the Law; and others set out, toward home or toward the next village, wherever, they carried bread and lard in a ragged bundle, carried bread and lard in their stomach, carried themselves through woods full of stillness, playing, daring, peeling away from the collective of dying bodies by assuming that they existed once again. They and not the collective. They were playing the game of individual.

Yes, the cats in the moonlight, and their yowling like the squeaking of the winch—what a funny word—, and yes, the well. Helen. Helen's arm, her neck, her legs, the vibrant body under her dress. A face. But he couldn't remember that face, he only knew (the way you know in the second year of junior high that Scandinavia is shaped like a yellow-and-brown striped tiger that is about to spring onto the continent), he only knew that it was roundish, slightly angular only along the jawbones, bright, the lips thin, the forehead high and straight as it flowed into the dark hair that was combed back smoothly; he saw this face as two-dimensional, as if it were separated from the head, pressed flat, an expanse of skin between two panes of glass. Helen at the well, Mrs. Wallach, wife of a railway man or a mailman named Veit Wallach, Veit in Latin is Vitus, he had to laugh about that, back then, in nineteen hundred and thirty-seven, the last Thennberg summer, Helen, Mrs. Vitus, she had a little son, no, a little daughter. She had almost fallen into the well, a wild little beast, golden blonde, no, straw blonde, no, wheaten blonde, no—finally the color radiated up—whitish blonde, of course, whitish blonde, like her father, skinny, a wild little thing all skin and bones with scabs on her bony knees, her name was Lilo. Go home, Helen had said, it was late in the afternoon, Lilo was tormenting the neutered tomcat in the courtyard, Vitus Wallach was in the train station or at the post office or in the pub, your mother will be worried, Helen had said. He didn't dare take her hand, that hand, now so strong, a few hours ago light as a feather, helping him out of his clothes, a few hours ago, an eternity ago; that hand had been like a bird, first lightly touching the skin with wing feathers, then clawing into the flesh. He turned and actually walked toward home. He couldn't bring himself to say that he would always, always and forever, for all eternity ... He heard her voice, far behind at his back, Lilo, she yelled, you dirty brat! An ox came toward him, dust swirled up behind the stone-colored hooves, not a soul was on the road, in the gardens dry leaves lay under the plane-trees, tattered, their edges curled up, Mother was sitting at the tea table playing solitaire, she really had been worried. And now tell us exactly what these breasts looked like de facto, Phoebus Silbermann had said, that had been way in the beginning, in the second concentration camp, or the third one, at any rate Markus Löw hadn't been around yet, they had still enjoyed talking about women then, some were still able to masturbate afterwards, yes, it had to be in the second camp, in the year nineteen hundred and thirty-nine. Phoebus Silbermann came from Stanislau, at one time the name Phoebus had been very fashionable there, he was an attorney specializing in patents for inventions about which he talked at length, a patron and silent partner of the inventors in hopes of becoming a millionaire someday, in the USA, with the help of gold-colored toothpaste, or a lighted pocket comb or a many-headed utility brush (which could be used as floor-, shoe-, and clothes brush), a thin little man, like a piece of cartilage covered with yellowish skin, quick, overbearing, interested in every little detail; for God does not live in the en gros, God lives in the detail, as Goethe said, declared Phoebus Silbermann, and then he added: If He lives, that is. An evening black as pitch. Somebody had started, with that kind of dirty talk, a long story in which the slightly flabby but nevertheless nicely rounded and at any rate enormous behind of a widowed vegetable hawker played the major role, then another voice came bubbling out of the heavy, chest-squeezing darkness, suddenly thighs shimmered as brightly as the alabaster-colored glass of church windows, shimmered, spread themselves, a hairy funnel opened up at the apex that sucked in all longings, and finally a third voice spoke, it told about Helen, a voice that he had listened to as if it hadn't been his own. Phoebus Silbermann had asked about details. And, stammering at first and searching for appropriate words, but then quite precisely, he had described the breasts, pear-shaped breasts with nipples that looked like a cross-eyed pair of eyes, solid upper arms, thick dark hair in the armpits that had the same odor as the hair around genitals that suggested a girl's mouth, the smiling mouth of a very young girl, but that smile was hidden behind thighs that were a bit heavy on the inside, a smile, by the way, that Helen's lips could never achieve, for even though they swelled up for a kiss, they were otherwise thin, hard lips in a stern face; between this face and the lower body there was a strange disproportion, a kind of hostility: The vibrant body had rebelled against the rigid, almost careworn face at every step, in every motion, at every moment, even when half asleep—that's about how he had described her, even though he no longer knew what she had really been like, Helen, after the gelatinous phantasies of masturbation his first lover.

In reality, he hadn't noticed the shape of her breasts or the hair in her armpits at that time, in Thennberg, in Vitus Wallach's double bed under the olograph which depicted Jesus Christ in white tunic and blue cloak on the moonlit Mount of Olives. If he had been aware of anything in his orgasmic spasms it had been his own inordinate desire and his own gasping breath and the fear of his own courage, of the awful virginity of his own body; what he had noticed was above all his amazement at the absolute shamelessness of his lover who seemed so calm, conscientious and matter-of-fact, who with housewifely motions pushed away the heavy down cover, took off her blouse, her skirt, in a matronly way stepped out of her slip, her panties, and finally lay down on the no longer clean sheet, there she lay waiting, motionless, dull, as if frozen in her dullness—that's what the reality looked like, was it really like that? He saw the image in the center of a block of ice, transparent as glass, and then he saw another image, and then a third one, Helen three times, the first time as she lay on the bed, motionless, under the olograph, the second time as he had described her at the request of Phoebus Silbermann (he later ended up at Auschwitz, ended up with a group there that collected newborn infants and hidden infants from the women's barracks and took them away on pushcarts—Adalbert Friedländer had seen him there with his own eyes), and now, since all of that had come up again, playfully raised to an inner light, a body to play with, now Helen had a third body, no longer surrounded by secrets, no longer object of hopes, free of lust; it was a body like any other body, a structure of wobbly flesh, a bag singularly formed out of the most delicate skin, covering bones, curved and straight, muscles mindlessly tensing and relaxing, soft organs. The back suggested a narrow coffin in which lay something still living. Perhaps Helen had died in a bomb explosion or was killed by a stray missile or an illness: only when he visualized her in the third image, dead, like all the dead bodies he had seen in the past years, only when the body lay lifeless, stiff, meaningless, helpless, only then was he home at last in that first love affair, and so home in Thennberg too. The open mouth of dead Adalbert Friedländer was at the same time the gasping open mouth of Helen Wallach, congealed in the middle of the gasp. Mouths, body openings, hairy bodies, hairless bodies, bodies: they slithered one over the other. And that too was a game.

The loamy yellow surface of a puddle curled under his foot, the water rose and fell again. Dried-up slices of bread rattled in his coat pocket. When they were all eaten up it would be time for the fish, for the brook, the rock and the fish. Some tree branches creaked. He saw a man who was looking at him.

Later, much later, the contractor Heinrich Moravec, in his deposition before the magistrate Doctor Zahidil, said roughly the following among other things:

I did not recognize him. One could say that I didn't want to recognize him, but that's not right. The last time I saw him he was thirteen or fourteen. That was in the year nineteen-hundred thirty-seven, Director Kranz and his family stayed at the manor-house every summer. That is, Director Kranz, his name was Ferdinand, wasn't there usually. He came on weekends or he didn't come at all. They said that he cheated on his wife. They said that he was drawn to foreign countries, to elegant spas, to the ocean. They said he begrudged himself vacations, that he was obsessed with making money. There were lots of rumors. His wife was an elegant lady but a little strange. She wasn't exactly crazy. But she wasn't quite right either. They said she wrote letters all the time, four or five every day. They said she never ate properly, that she lived mostly on tea and cookies. She stayed up very late every night. At two in the morning the lights were still on at the manor-house. Sometimes she wanted to use the telephone at night. When that happened she sent the maid to the post office. The maid had to get up in the middle of the night to go to the post office, and then the postmaster had to get up, because there's no other connection here at night. His name was Veit Wallach, he fell in Russia. (I myself didn't have to serve; due to a hunting accident at age nineteen my left leg is shorter than my right leg by six centimeters.) The fact that I married Wallach's widow is documented. She died in nineteen hundred forty-three of stomach cancer. Her daughter by her first marriage, Liselotte Wallach, was thirteen at the time. By then her name was Moravec. I will come back to her later. So her father, Veit Wallach, would get out of bed, go to the post office, and make the connection so Mrs. Kranz could do her telephoning. He got paid for this, plenty, they said. Mrs. Kranz usually talked to a lady in Zurich. Wallach said that the lady in Zurich was Mrs. Kranz's sister. He used to listen in. Maybe he just said that to conceal the real state of affairs. As a courtesy, so to speak. He took money, after all. They said that Mrs. Kranz was in love with the lady in Zurich. A soul friendship, such a thing can happen between women. Or lesbians. Makes no difference. De mortuis nil nisi bene. Once, maybe in thirty-five, the Zurich lady stayed at the manor-house too. During those weeks Director Kranz happened to be present also. Maybe the lady from Zurich was his lover. There are supposed to be cases where a man can live with two women at the same time, and the two women get along fine that way. Too well. I simply can't imagine such a thing, but with people like the Kranz family there could be all kinds of goings-on.

The manor-house where they lived isn't really a manor-house, we just called it that because it used to belong to old Baron Ammer. Then it belonged to his son. Now it belongs to me.

We never saw the young baron. Hardly ever. He had a face that you couldn't remember: Rosy complexion, round chin, gray eyes. He wore checkered suits. He had a soft little voice. He had a cold all the time. Later he was a Nazi. His father is buried in our cemetery. When his son joined the Nazis, the old man probably turned over in his grave. Old Baron Ammer was a gentleman.

The house he rented to Director Kranz is very imposing, but a manor-house it isn't. In the summer months Baron Ammer stayed at a hunting lodge in a forest glade on Mount Eichel. In the winter he lived in the manor-house. That's what killed him: pneumonia. But in the summer months you could live quite nicely at the manor-house. It was relatively dry. So that is where Mrs. Kranz lived, and the son too, of course.

The first time I saw him was in nineteen hundred thirty-five, before the Zurich lady came to visit. He was maybe twelve. A child. I didn't have the business yet at that time, but I was already in construction. There was always something to build at the manor-house. For instance, before the lady from Zurich came to visit, the loft was refurbished. We remodeled it into an attic, we built a whole little apartment, it was very nice. Like a doll house. How Director Kranz who was just renting could have been permitted to have a house remodeled that didn't even belong to him I don't know. Maybe he had bought the house from the old Baron. Later on it didn't make any difference, because the Jews were purged, and after that the house belonged to the young baron.

At that time I worked in the office of the construction company, because I had to interrupt my studies. My parents ran out of money, and I was only in my fifth semester. I had wanted to be a pharmacist, that's a secure life, and our pharmacist wasn't the youngest anymore. The pharmacy is pretty old too. Our village is small but we still have a pharmacy. There are two reasons for that. First, there were times when Thennberg was of some importance. Back then there was a famous market here once a week. We had a post office and a surveying station here too. Secondly, Old Baron Ammer's great-grandfather was a nut. He was crazy about the simple folk and he was crazy about himself. He was a hypochondriac. So Thennberg got a pharmacy. At that time, when I was studying pharmacology, the pharmacist had a daughter by the name of Katherina whom I wanted to marry at any cost. When I went into the building trade she married somebody else. His name is Erich Mohaupt and he runs the pharmacy today. He is an alderman too. This Mohaupt snatched Katherina away from me. His father was a judge, although close to retirement, but at any rate he was in the civil service. Judge Mohaupt and old Baron Ammer were school friends. The old pharmacist belonged to their clique. The gentlemen had a thing going. And I didn't have the money to go to school. If it hadn't been for this experience in my youth I would not be what I am today.

When I came to the manor-house at that time in thirty-five, I saw the young Kranz for the first time. He was fat and melancholy. I still remember thinking: a boy that age ought to be racing around, but this one just sits in an easy chair with a book, or else he walks up and down under the trees like an old man. I thought: degenerate without a doubt; no wonder, congenitally afflicted.

That was a whole different constellation then. My later wife, as I said, was still married to Veit Wallach. Liselotte was only five and Richard only twelve. The children grow up but the old ones don't die right away. They have to live with each other. That leads to complications.

So Richard Kranz came again with his mother the next summer and the summer after that. He was on vacation. The rest of the time he went to a prep school in Vienna. He showed an unusual interest in country-life. He tried to talk to boys his age from the village, which was not customary. He also went to mass every Sunday even though he was a Jew, born a Jew at least. Maybe the members of the Kranz family had themselves baptized. Maybe young Kranz considered himself a Christian. But still it wasn't right for him to go to mass.

He had a notebook in which he wrote down all words and phrases that were new to him. He liked everything rustic. We used to laugh about it. There was a tennis court on the manor grounds. Although young Kranz looked lazy he played tennis regularly, either with his governess or with Erich Mohaupt. One day Richard Kranz came on the tennis court with his notebook and asked the ball boys to tell him rustic idioms. Folklore. The ball boys were children of the poorest people. When they didn't want to say anything, Richard Kranz promised them ten Groschen for every word that he didn't know. After that he got to hear words that were sure new to him. He wrote them all down in his notebook. Our language here is limited. The ball boys had nothing better to offer than words for genital organs, all the words that describe the sex act, in other words, things that normally were not mentioned in Vienna among refined people. Or only among men. Richard Kranz paid. Then he wanted to know what the words meant, but nobody had the nerve to explain the meaning of these words. He went to the governess with his notebook. The governess alerted Mrs. Kranz. After that young Kranz didn't come on the tennis court for a while. Then he played again as if nothing had happened. But he avoided the village boys from then on.

It was better that way because everybody just laughed at him. Maybe he appeared normal in his normal milieu. In the village he seemed ridiculous. They said he was nearsighted but that he was too vain to wear glasses. They said his skin was so delicate he could only wear ladies' underwear. They said the village boys lay in wait for him in the woods and beat him up and he didn't defend himself and never told anyone. They said he wasn't a real boy because he was in love with Erich Mohaupt.

As a matter of fact, the two could be seen together a lot, not just on the tennis court. Judge Mohaupt and his son lived modestly. They said: old Baron Ammer rented the manor house to the Kranz family and Judge Mohaupt didn't have a manor house, so he rented them his son. That's about how most people saw it. Director Kranz was very rich. He knew the right people in Vienna. The connection with Richard Kranz could be useful to Erich Mohaupt. But Richard Kranz stood to gain nothing by his friendship with Erich Mohaupt. So he had to have a secret reason, probably a dirty one, for being so devoted to Erich Mohaupt. His enthusiasm for everything rustic was no explanation because Erich Mohaupt wasn't a peasant. There was the possibility, of course, that the two were just friends. But that would have been too simple. And besides: people like the Kranzes would have no idea about such a thing as selfless friendship, since they act only according to their own self-interest. Only people to whom feelings, true feelings, are nothing but a dispensable luxury, only such people get rich.

In the summer of thirty-seven we stopped laughing about Richard Kranz. We started to hate him. And it wasn't just the times, I mean the anti-Semitism, but it was a new story. Perhaps this new story wouldn't have attracted so much attention if Richard Kranz hadn't been a Jew, a Jew, no matter how often he went to mass. But the state of affairs being what it was, the thing turned into a scandal. I think Richard Kranz wasn't even aware of the scandal. After all, people didn't talk to him anymore after that, and then summer vacation came to an end, he went home again and didn't come back, or rather, not until the spring of forty-five, and things were different then. I personally have to be thankful to young Kranz for this scandal, because as a result I was able to marry Helen and to have Liselotte by my side after her death.

So they talked about how Richard Kranz wasn't as dumb as he made out, not as unworldly, since he managed to start an affair with Veit Wallach's wife. They talked about how Mrs. Wallach had taken money for it, and plenty of it too. There were even people who said that she had done a smart thing, for the Post Office paid miserably, and the Wallachs had a child after all. But most of them were down on it. They expressed their opinion quite vigorously, in fact. Supposedly somebody saw Mrs. Wallach and young Kranz disappear, not into the manor-house but into her own house. Supposedly somebody heard that the door had been bolted. Somebody said Mrs. Wallach had first taken Liselotte to the neighbors indicating that they should watch the child because she had been suffering from a headache for some time and needed desperately to go to the pharmacy. Somebody said she never was at the pharmacy. Somebody saw Mrs. Wallach come out of her house with young Kranz in the late afternoon. She had obviously fetched Liselotte home earlier because the child was playing in the courtyard.

Two weeks later Veit Wallach bought himself a motorcycle. He said he had saved up, and some people actually remembered that he had planned to buy a motorcycle. But memories get easily confused. The greater the hope for a full-fledged scandal, the easier the confusion. I said before that the scandal couldn't be blamed on the times alone. That is true. There would have been a scandal even if Richard Kranz hadn't been a Jew and a fourteen-year-old one at that. Presumably the scandal would just have been a lesser one. I knew that Mrs. Wallach drove the men crazy. She had nothing to do with it, just the way she looked and the way she carried herself. She drove me crazy too, and so I married her after Wallach was killed.

He was the only one who forgave her the business with young Kranz. No, he didn't really forgive it: he refused to believe that he had been deceived. I was there myself when they told him the story. That was in the pub. Wallach had taken a test drive on the motorcycle, and then he had invited his friends to celebrate the new vehicle. We drank plenty. We are used to drinking a lot. We drank to the motorcycle and to Veit Wallach, we drank to Veit Wallach's good fortune, and finally somebody couldn't resist the well-meaning candor of calling this good fortune by name. That one drank to the health of Richard Kranz. The others drank along, only I didn't drink along and Wallach didn't either, of course. And since I was the only one who didn't drink along he looked at me. I said: here's to you! He asked: Young Kranz? Somebody said: C'mon, don't pretend. Wallach asked once more: Young Kranz? I said nothing. Somebody said: There, there, Veit, here's to your long life. Innkeeper, another liter! Wallach still had a broad smile on his face. He liked to laugh. Then his smile disappeared, and very shortly he said: You can kiss my ass, all of you. Then he sat down, for he had been standing until then. I think nobody heard what he said, because they were all busy with themselves, having their own good time. With the titillating thought that somebody had managed to do it to

Helen, even if it was the young Kranz who certainly had to pay plenty for it; a motorcycle had its price after all. But I didn't laugh. For I loved my later wife already then. And so I heard what Vitus Wallach had said very softly.

Later he was jovial again, because he had thought it over and he didn't believe that Helen had deceived him, and still later he was quite drunk, like the rest of us.

It was insane to think that Helen could have had an affair with Richard Kranz. It was the times. Wallach never believed in his wife's guilt, although the last four years of that marriage probably weren't all that happy. Otherwise Helen wouldn't have married me so quickly, just like that, after the message came that her husband had fallen on the eastern front. We had a good marriage. It lasted only two years, but they were harmonious ones. Only once did I ask my wife openly and clearly how that gossip could have started. I used to throw out hints about it all the time but only once did I ask. She said: I could have fallen in love with that boy, but I'm sorry to say, all he did was bring me a book to read, a French novel, but that wouldn't make any difference to any of you because you don't read books anyway. She must have been very upset to say something like that to me. Because she certainly knew that I am rather well read. No wonder she was upset. The scandal had gotten under her skin, and all the time she had to pretend that she didn't notice anything. So then I didn't ask again. She needed to forget that whole business. Then she died. And on her death bed? She had nothing to confess. At first she had to go through the tortures of hell, but then she just lay there.

Her mouth was open, her breathing was labored and got weaker all the time. Her lower jaw dropped. She held her legs spread out a little. Sometimes they made walking motions, jerking in the knee joints. Her two arms lay there, to the right and left, with the little sores left by the injection needles, withered, like spider legs. Her head seemed to have gotten smaller. Her chest with the lovely bosom still arched up. Her complexion was yellowish. The lines around her mouth were deep. The curve of her nose was more pronounced than before; the waxiness began at the nose. There were tubes stuck in her nostrils, and oxygen flowed through them.

I must apologize for this detailed description. But I really did love my wife, however childish that may sound, and I continued to love her in her daughter; I want to confess to this feeling.

I didn't see young Kranz again then. I saw him for the last time in late August of nineteen hundred thirty-seven and then again eight years later in the spring of forty-five.

I went to the woods at that time, to get firewood. Everybody did that, one has to heat and cook after all. Liselotte had been given two rabbits by Judge Mohaupt, who was being provided for by the former gamekeeper of Baron Ammer may God rest his soul. I sold one of the rabbits to a lady from Vienna. I didn't know her. She gave a Bucharian rug for the rabbit. That sort of thing was customary then. Liselotte planned to roast the other rabbit. I went to get wood. I went by myself. I wasn't afraid because there weren't any Russians in our village, and anyway I was carrying my pistol. That's when I saw a man who was dressed in rags, but not ordinary rags. You could tell from the rags where they came from. They came from the concentration camp. So the man was a former C-camper. He was young but in very bad condition. They hardly had anything to eat in the concentration camp, especially toward the end. They had no heat. The people died like flies. We knew all that. The camp wasn't very far from our village. It was the only C-camp in the area. I knew it from before. There used to be a cement factory there, but it burned down later, and they built the barracks from the rubble and from other materials. The company that I was with was in on the construction. It wasn't a big job, but at least it was a job.

So the C-camper stood on the path in the woods. I knew immediately that I would persuade him to stay at my house. It was a good deed, but I didn't think about that then. I thought that I would take this C-camper into our house so he could protect us if necessary. It was the times. One had to be prepared for anything: for the Russians, for the new government, for acts of revenge, for crimes, for violence. Liselotte was fifteen. It was my duty to protect her. A house in which a former C-camper lived was the safest I could offer her.

He seemed a bit confused. He asked if the road really led to Thennberg. I asked: Thennberg? Why Thennberg? He took a piece of bread with lard out of his pocket and gave me half of it. I gave him a cigarette. Then we walked home, very slowly. Liselotte roasted the rabbit. The C-camper slept upstairs, in the bedroom that hadn't been used since the death of my wife. (I slept in a little room downstairs at the time, and my daughter Lilo had the living room.)

Only later, when we were sitting at the table, did he say that he was Richard Kranz. I wouldn't have recognized him.

She had known that he would come to visit her, her particularly, even though he couldn't possibly remember her, and she also knew that the visit was not meant for her but for her husband of whom she had had no news for more than a year, maybe he was dead even as his boyhood friend suddenly appeared out of nowhere, Richard Kranz, who wouldn't be able to remember her at all and who would remember all the others whom he had encountered here only as in a dream, and even that dream would have to be meaningless to him, like a picture postcard, "Lovely days in Thennberg." She had also known that he would not come to see her at home, in her father-in-law's house, but in the pharmacy during business hours. There was much that she knew, and sometimes she wondered how she knew all that, how other people's carefully guarded secrets flew to her just like that, silly little schoolgirls' secrets and weighty secrets such as those her father-in-law had when he had kept other books hidden behind his law books, books by Schnitzler and Kraus and Altenberg and Friedell and all those names, and the heaviest secrets, even secrets that one could never say out loud and could hardly even think, like Lilo's secret, Lilo who one day had burst in and had first talked around it but then, not even embarrassed but rather with pride had told it all —everything seemed to rush toward her, she didn't know why, every once in a while she had the notion that she was like a center of gravity. This time the visit was not meant for the center of gravity but for her husband, and through him for her as well. Lilo had announced the visit, on the evening of the day Richard Kranz had arrived; wrapped in kerchiefs, muffled up, unrecognizable, she flew through the open door, it was already evening, out of the darkness she scampered into the dimly lit hall. Heinz brought the young Kranz, she said breathlessly, tossing one of the kerchiefs on the chair, pushing the other one to the side. Who is here? Old Mohaupt asked from the room. Imagine, said Lilo, Heinz is beside himself, it's written all over his face, I don't care if he puts on the dignified gentleman act, he's beside himself just the same, and after dinner young Kranz asked about Erich, and we told him that he had got married, married to you, and that he had gone to the front then, and then he said right away that he would come to see you, right away tomorrow morning, in the pharmacy, he said he could find the way to the pharmacy on his own, third street on the left, opposite the church, there used to be cough drops displayed in the window in glass jars.

She had looked at Lilo without saying anything. She delighted in her and admired her, this thin blond girl with the pointed nose, with the lively, pale lips, with the pretty little figure, this excited little person who used to address pharmacist Erich Mohaupt simply as Erich although he was thirteen years older than this chatterbox, a little woman with red cheeks, too red, maybe tubercular, who said whatever came into her head, brazen and yet virginal, like a pretty little animal, who didn't say father, or stepfather, or Heinrich Moravec or Herr Moravec or just Moravec in God's name, but simply: Heinz. Not everywhere. But here, where she had got rid of her heavy secret, here Lilo said: Heinz. Maybe her secret didn't seem heavy to her at all, maybe she wasn't at all proud of it but thought it only natural that she had replaced her dead mother not only as housekeeper but in the bed as well. Come on in, old Mohaupt called from the room, and Lilo flew right on, from the hall to the easy chair and from the easy chair to the sofa, in between stepping very close to the old man and looking into his eyes without kissing his bald head, for she had long since understood that Mohaupt did not want to be kissed. And there she had sat, totally blank, well-behaved, as if in church, had talked about this and that, and then had left with all her kerchiefs, had faded from the light into the darkness, and her heels had drummed loudly and merrily on the cobble-stones of the garden path.

    She, the pharmacist's wife, Katherina Mohaupt, thought to herself, a bit enviously but then again really without envy but forgivingly and admiringly and almost benevolently: A splendid girl. She couldn't stand this generosity of hers. It made life difficult, made everything complicated. It was like a pet that terrorized her. She felt fine most of the time, even when she had to look at evil. She was filled to overflowing with good health. Just this goodness was something she couldn't cope with. It stung like a burr in the behind.

So she had known that he would come to pay a visit to the wife of his best friend, but then, when he had actually come she had nothing to offer him but a sympathetic, an all-too sympathetic silence that must have enveloped him comfortably but isolated him as well. Do you have any news about Erich? No. Had he still played tennis? Yes, at the manor house, I played too. Are you a good player? Pretty good. I learned a lot from him. Really? Nietzsche and Stefan George and Ernst Jünger, we were kids after all. He talked a lot about you. Really? Really. That was about how the conversation went. An old woman came in with a prescription. Phenylethylbarbituric acid, hydrochlorocodeine, caffeine, Dimapyrin, phenacetin. You could not get codeine anymore. The old woman had left again. A little schnapps? No alcohol, please, three days ago the Russians . . . Was that terrible? The conversation had trickled along. Then Richard Kranz asked: Do you think that I would be allowed to have a look at the manor house?

She nodded. Nobody is living at the manor house, she told him, the last tenant, a man by the name of Joachim Schwarzer, had disappeared long ago, and Richard Kranz could go there, and if he wanted to go through the rooms, nobody would stop him. But while she was nodding her head, horribly long and all-too sympathetically, she suddenly saw Mrs. Kranz before her, in a black silk dress with large peach-colored flowers, a wide-brimmed straw hat on her head, standing under the plane-trees between two massive tree trunks, their thin bark hanging down in palm-sized patches. The woman in the black silk dress was standing in the foliage. A second woman in a dress the color of tired tea roses came up to the first woman and handed hea letter. The scene was totally without sound. Katherina Mohaupt thought: like a ballet. Then, another scene, a large green car with white-walled tires drove up. A servant set two suitcases down in the dust next to the running board that was covered with faintly gleaming grooved rubber. The suitcases were made of pigskin and had brightly colored papers pasted all over them. The chauffeur was sweating. He took off his flat gray cap and wiped the sweat from his forehead with a checkered handkerchief. Mrs. Kranz got into the car and sat down, this time she was wearing a dove-gray suit. The other lady, again the color of tea roses, sat down next to her. A little later young Kranz came with his governess. She was gaunt. He walked very slowly, as though he were moving his plump, slightly reddish thighs with great difficulty. His face was round and white, his dark eyes resembled two cherries that from a distance seemed to glow although they merely reflected sparks of light. Strangely veiled eyes. The car had driven away, and the dust cloud settled down. And she was still nodding her head. He said: Let me know right away when Erich comes home, I beg of you. And then he asked: Is it possible that I know Miss Moravec from before? But that's impossible, he added immediately, because I never knew Mr. Moravec, and so I couldn't have known his daughter, and anyway, she must have been very little way back then, right? How old might she be? I figure seventeen, or not quite seventeen. A beautiful girl and so clean, it sounds silly, I know, but Miss Moravec is really beautiful and so totally innocent, yes, so clean, he repeated, and then he said once more: let me know right away when Erich comes home. She said: For God's sake, leave, let me have your address and I'll be sure to let you know, he'll surely write to you right away, but go somewhere else, go and take a look at the manor house, there's nobody living at the manor house now, a gentleman from Constance was the last one who lived at the manor house, you don't know him, a German, his name was Joachim Schwarzer, take a rest, I'll give you some medications, whatever we have around, get back on your feet, but then go away immediately. He asked: Why?

It was just twelve o'clock noon, Ambrose, the limping, half-crazy sexton's substitute, was yanking the rope around in the church tower, and the bell boomed, you couldn't have heard an answer, and there was no answer anyway, instead of an answer the yellowish, home-brewed plum brandy quivered in the two little glasses, Richard Kranz raised his politely, she raised hers, looked at it and then poured the schnapps down her throat, cheers, she said afterwards, and he raised his glass, touched the schnapps with his tongue and said: Cheers. Then he asked: Why should I leave right away? I have to get some sleep first. Then I have to go to the church too, to see Father Horowitz, if he's still alive. I'd like to get to the manor house too. I always had such a good time here in Thennberg, as a boy I used to look forward all year to summer when I could be in Thennberg at last, going for walks, playing tennis with Erich, I even fell in love here, in Thennberg, I was fourteen then, and it was a secret. Nobody knew about it, that I was in love, even she—I wouldn't want to mention her name—didn't know. I asked about her, and Mr. Moravec told me that she had died. At the camp, I mean, here, in the last C-camp, I sometimes thought to myself: How strange, Thennberg must be close by here, I could simply take a stroll there, and now I am actually here. Isn't that funny? He spoke softly and slowly, as though he had to look for the words and gather them together with great difficulty, or as though he wanted to savor this, the casual, aimless chatter to the wife of his friend. And then he asked once more: So tell me, why should I leave right away?

Like a little ball of lead the answer lay in her skull, it hurt her, it wanted to get out, and why not, he had to find out sometime. She looked at him. He was very thin, his face had a yellowish color; perhaps he was ill. She felt her dangerous weakness, that awful softness rising from the region of her stomach which trembled with agitation. The attack of goodness spread through her body. She controlled herself, didn't give in. She couldn't tell him that she knew everything, that the love affair between Helen Wallach and young Kranz had been common knowledge, she couldn't bring herself to reveal to him that Heinrich Moravec had married Helen and then, after Helen's death, had started a sexual relationship with Lilo; it was better for Richard Kranz not to know any of this and to go away, as quickly as possible. Was it really better? Was it really empathy and goodness that constricted her throat, or was it an unspoken law of solidarity with all the other people here who knew everything and did not speak out, was it the cronyism of a native conspiracy? She was silent. Then she said: I thought you'd want to see if your parents . . . she could not utter the word "died," and so that she didn't have to say anything more she refilled the little glasses.

He picked up his glass immediately, raised it to his mouth in one quick motion, drank, returned it to the bare glass top of the counter, then he looked at her. He grinned. He said: Well, it isn't really all that important, but my parents are no longer living. It must have been difficult for him to form the words, for his lips remained stretched out as he uttered that sentence, frozen into a grin. She said: I'm very sorry. But as she said this she felt how idiotic that was, how mechanical, how hollow, and so she added: I admired your mother, I mean when I was a little girl. He nodded and pushed the empty schnapps glass toward her which she filled a third time, and so as not to be impolite she filled hers at the same time. He drank. Then he said: You must be younger than me but a few years older than Miss Moravec; I am twenty-two and so Erich must be twenty-six, and you, let me guess, twenty? She nodded even though she was twenty-two as well, but she didn't want to contradict him, and besides, he really did look much older; she had married Erich at eighteen, and soon thereafter he had gone into the service, and she had the feeling that she hadn't changed since then, but Richard Kranz, who was again reaching for the schnapps glass, leaning back in the white-painted chair rather helplessly, tired or perhaps a little drunk by now, Richard Kranz was no longer young, he looked to be around thirty. She was still nodding, and as she nodded she thought, Lilo has driven him crazy in that one day, without meaning to, in fun, out of coquettishness—for she was absolutely and totally honest, that Lilo, without ulterior motives, and just because of that it wasn't her fault that something in her was always flirting: with the pots that she stirred, with the clouds she watched as they passed, and naturally also with the men—and Richard Kranz was no longer that melancholy boy with the fat behind but a gaunt man, starved, nothing but skin and bones. He needed to be nurtured so that he could forget, needed to be fed light foods, needed to be spoiled as he had been spoiled as a boy, Richard Kranz needed his mother, or he needed a woman who could be a mother to him as well, for he was, although apparently in good physical shape, moribund. He was walking around unsuspecting, but in reality he was on his death-bed. She recognized his death as it lay in his eyes, now no longer so veiled, not without their own light as they had been back then, she saw the dying, his dying, in the greed with which he poured the schnapps into his throat. After he had finished the fifth glass he said: I will not leave immediately. Do you know what I'm going to do? I'm going to pay court to Miss Moravec. And after the eighth glass he said: I will pay court to her first of all because the expression is so nice, paying court, and secondly because for five years I could have died every day, was supposed to die if the authorities had had their wish, and thirdly because Thennberg for me is . . . He drank. Then he didn't say anything for a long time.

He left then. May I come again? he asked. She nodded.

After he had gone she rinsed her mouth. Then she mixed the powder for the old woman. Afterwards she closed up the pharmacy and went to the cemetery, to her father's grave. She visited this grave rather frequently. She lit a candle stub in the wrought-iron lantern, said a prayer, with a branch she smoothed the clumps of earth into which she would put some seeds when warm weather came, and not until she was on the way home did she realize that she had prayed not for her father's salvation but for the salvation of Richard Kranz.

Let's be merry, let's be gay, the worst thing that can happen is death, and that isn't all that horrible either, but anyway, death is still a little distance away; if everything goes wrong there's always the brook and the rock and the fish, and things aren't anywhere near as bad as that, maybe they'll never be that bad, five glasses of schnapps can't do any harm to a Richard Kranz, no way, long enough did he eat gruel, for breakfast, for lunch, for dinner, he got gruel with bacterial cultures from the Nazis, then bread and lard and schnapps from the Russians, ten glasses of schnapps could not hurt a Richard Kranz, ten glasses of gray schnapps in a gray pharmacy, pictures of little schnapps glasses in the picture of a pharmacy; myself, Anna Csillag, yes, Anna Csillag in person, with her enormous seventy-three-inch long Lorelei-hair, standing behind the counter selling mustache wax from a box that is painted on the wall, and next to Anna Csillag stands Katherina Mohaupt, also painted on the wall with colors made of wax; let's be merry, let's be gay, what's his name, yes, the name was Joachim Schwarzer, he lived in the manor house, and he had come up from Constance, but now he was gone, nobody lived at the manor house, at most Mother came back every once in a while, to creak a bit behind the closed doors of the wardrobe, provided this wardrobe was still in existence, and Father walked up and down in the attic, in Aunt Paula's little apartment, every once in a while, when he felt like it, he would do a pirouette, one to the left, then one to the right and then another one to the left—come, Miss Moravec, let's go visit my parents. This chill in your bones is not a true chill, I can feel it too, that's just the schnapps, it was a bit cool, it was gray too, you could tell the chill by looking at it. It can't be cold, the sun is shining, Reverend Horowitz had them ring the bells an hour ago, two at the most. It is spring, it's in the afternoon, little flowers are blooming, listen, Miss Moravec, the mill goes clickety-clack in the babbling brook, if it were cold it couldn't go clickety-clack, the brook would be frozen over.

    I never saw it frozen over, and the meadows had been a summery green, and then, toward the end of vacation, they had been yellowish, always green and yellowish, the plane trees always in leaf, it had never occurred to me that there would be winter in Thennberg, and I don't know how the people dress then—do they wear long coats or sheepskins, clogs or boots, hoods made of felt or lambskin caps, do they celebrate slaughter festivals, do they go to midnight mass on Christmas eve, do they get together at the pub, do they go to bed as soon as it gets dark, do they have balls, dances, fancy-dress affairs, do they hate each other because they have nothing better to do, do they badmouth the foreigners who could be seen behind the windows of the speeding express train as it thundered by every evening, never stopping in Thennberg, do they grumble about the overdressed women, about the stingy old folks, about the government, about the Jews who are always causing trouble, do they drink beer or wine or schnapps? Maybe there was always winter in Thennberg, and just when I was there it was summer, in passing, for a moment, and as soon as I looked the other way it began to snow again, and icicles hung from people's noses; Erich Mohaupt, the only winter person from Thennberg, I didn't see him in Thennberg but in Vienna, in the snow-covered passageway between Michaelerplatz and Habsburgergasse, there, under the memorial plaque of the musicologist and composer Franz Krenn, we used to meet, by the yellow light of the shop windows, for we lived in Brunerstrasse, and Mohaupt had taken a room in Lange Gasse, be came to meet me, but only as far as the passage, rarely did he come up to our apartment. But here, in Thennberg, he didn't have a problem, he came to the manor house almost every day.

Well, here we are, here is the manor house, Miss Moravec, take a look at this rocker, somewhat displaced, it sits in the dust, in front of the entrance, and the seat and the back are in shreds, but it doesn't matter, in this rocker Uncle Edi used to sit, Edward Kranz of Anglo-Danubia, he wore a suit of immaculate white linen and a shirt of yellowish silk and a straw hat with a wide brim and shoes that were brown in front and white at the top, he ordered his ties from Turkey, for he wore only ties with a Turkish motif, and neither in Olmtz nor in Reichenberg were they able to copy this pattern properly, he was a bachelor and he smoked cigars, he didn't light them until after he had bitten off the tightly rolled pointed end, even though he owned a cigar-cutter which he carried in his left vest pocket, Edi Kranz, they even knew him in the London Central, in the City. Every time Uncle Edi said the word City he would spit the end of the cigar into a big, pot-bellied Chinese vase that stood in the corner in spitting distance from the rocker.

The Chinese vase had been a gift from Aunt Paula. She lived in Zurich and she was permanently unhappy. Come, Miss Moravec, come on, I will show you the Chinese vase, it is in the parlor, no, I was wrong, it isn't in the parlor, for clearly there is no longer a parlor, which will surely not surprise you, Miss Moravec, since you are, after all, not present either, you are presently residing in a world where all those who are not yet here or will never be here reside, perhaps you are in the parlor right now, looking at the Chinese vase. It was a gift from Aunt Paula who was depressed because she had hoped that Father would marry her, but Father had not married Aunt Paula but her older sister, although that older sister had already reconciled herself to the idea of taking the veil, not the veil of a nun, of course, but that other, shorter veil that women wore in front of their face when they wanted to be elegant or else when they didn't want to be easily recognizable; such a veil had dangled in front of Mother's face, she was already ensconced in a bachelor flat, ran around with Bulgarian doctors or with French painters and sometimes just with quaint females who were interested in psychoanalysis or in kinesthetics or in Rudolf Steiner or in Marxism or in African music and sometimes in all of those. Her name had been Rombach then, Elfriede Rombach, she had studied medicine for a few semesters, she did what she wanted, her father paid for everything, the shipper Jacob Rombach, born in a village near Lemberg, delivery contractor in Vienna, at the time of his death he had eighteen bicycles and three automobiles on the road plus he owned two apartment houses and a racing stable in Freudenau to boot.

When he was a little boy he, Jacob Rombach, had been taken to Hungary, to the little town of Vc or Waizen that had a triumphal arch and a prison and a weekly outdoor market between the two; the parents of Jacob Rombach died in Vc, he was eight or nine years old, went to live with some distant relatives who let him stay with them for appearance's sake, but they didn't send him to school and didn't have him learn a proper trade either; so he just hung around, in Vc, at the market, he just stood there because he didn't have anything better to do than to stand there and to gaze helplessly into thin air. And suddenly he saw a tent, the kind they often had at such markets. Next to the entrance to the tent hung a notice on which it said that here, for very little money, one could obtain help with all of life's problems, and since he was helpless he went in and told the man who sat behind a table he should give him some advice, any advice at all, only it couldn't cost more than two pennies. The man took the two pennies and said: For two pennies I advise you to bend way down when you wash your hands or else the water will run into your sleeves. Jacob Rombach thanked him, went away, and became a rich man on the basis of this advice, for from then on he took whatever money anybody gave him, no matter how little, just as the man in the tent had done, and gave in return exactly the value of the money, never more, but never less either, gave it politely and earnestly, he behaved as that man in the tent had behaved, a mature man, his hair already graying, to a nine-year old boy. And so he was later able to buy a bachelor flat for his older daughter when she didn't care about getting married, and here Ferdinand Kranz, who was really wooing the younger daughter, went astray because he, too, was interested in psychoanalysis and in kinesthetics and in Rudolf Steiner and in Marxism and in African music. He was a bank clerk.

Paula usually stayed home as was proper, playing the piano in the large, dusky apartment of the late Jakob Rombach. Elfriede was by then occupied with preparing cadaver sections. She had also cheerfully made the decision that, if absolutely necessary, she would sacrifice her life for the sake of freedom for the human race, while Paula was in love with only one man, Ferdinand Kranz.

Much later she married into a singing school in Zurich, where she continued to play the piano while her husband managed the business, a handsome Italian, once an opera singer with nodes on his vocal chords, nodes that eventually turned out to be the first signs of incipient cancer of the throat. The singing school belonged to a Swiss rug merchant, who was an opera fan. After her husband's death he supported Aunt Paula, it was said that he was hopelessly in love with her, but perhaps he only hoped to be hopelessly in love, because Aunt Paula was too decent, much too conscientious not to give something in return for the emolument which she received every month, something that to give would be of relatively little trouble to her—but one could only guess at that and after all, the whole affair wasn't anybody's business, only Edward Kranz displayed a tiny grain of knowledge as he spat the bitten-off tip of his cigar into Aunt Paula's gift with the words: A gosh-awful pot, but at least acquired with the fruits of honest labor.

Mother didn't like such talk; the cadavers which she had dissected in her youth had floated out of her memory, bobbing up and down in formaldehyde, psychoanalysis had shrunk to the subject of learned conversation, kinesthetics, Rudolf Steiner, Marxism and African music meant about as much to her as a dried, pressed flower in a prayer book would mean to other women her age; and so Mother withdrew to her bedroom, come, Miss Moravec, take a look at the bedroom, it's all right, the shutters are still in working condition, there is even an office chair, but that wasn't around then, or at least not in this room, but there, in the corner, where you can see three piles of dog poop, that's where the bed stood, in the style of Louis the Fourteenth or Louis the Sixteenth, there was a dispute about this off and on, I myself believe that it didn't have a thing to do with any Louis, but it's all the same; so Mother lay in this bed, the lamp on the bedside table had a honey-colored silk shade, the light fell onto a book, Mother read novels before going to sleep, always a few pages from two different novels on the same evening, first something by Marcel Proust, perhaps, or by Colette, and then a mystery. She always slept with the window open, and when Uncle Edi came to visit she had to read a great deal more than usual before she could finally go to sleep because when the weather was fine Uncle Edi would sit at the table under the plane trees until way after midnight and regale his cronies with the wildest stories about some peasants or businessmen in Slovenia, Croatia or way down in Bosnia who had tried to put one over on the representatives of Anglo-Danubia with the craftiest tricks, and they would have been able to carry it off just like that if he hadn't been there, he, Eduard Kranz, he laughed, roared with laughter, and his cronies roared with laughter too, and Mother sought refuge from this laughter in Charlie Chan or Sherlock Holmes.

Or she took off, long before vacation was over, she didn't inform Father until after her departure and she didn't tell Uncle Edi at all, he was still asleep, he slept way into the morning, and she would simply not be there, she had kept this much of her youthful radicalism; she went off, at a moment's notice, as though to join a Bulgarian doctor or a French painter, and her long silk shawl which she wore for traveling draped snugly around her neck and trailing down to her knees in the manner of the dancer Isadora Duncan, fluttered in the backdraft of the open automobile, a banner of feminine emancipation. This shawl ought to be around somewhere, I'd like to give it to you, Miss Moravec, do you see a shawl anywhere? It isn't here, and you aren't here, that being the case, you can obviously see it; it is yours. Put it around your neck and then let one end hang down, but be careful, don't step on the free end, you could strangle yourself that way, your neck is very thin, just as thin as Agnes Deutsch's neck—yes, well, so Mother took off, and I sat next to her on a little seat, my governess sat opposite. Her name was Margot, and her hair was always neatly combed. We drove to Abbazia.

In Abbazia all the trees were in bloom all the time, but it was a tired sort of bloom, reminiscent of the taste of the orange marmalade that was on the breakfast table every morning in a round glass jar, together with the square slices of toasted wheat bread, every morning it looked like yesterday's marmalade in yesterday's glass jar, for none of us ever ate any orange marmalade; the curled strips of orange peel congealed in reddish honey-colored jelly looked like worms, the marmalade was caked, it had a dull glaze, getting duller all the time, and the thick petals in Abbazia hung from their stems like handkerchiefs, heavy and fleshy, too fleshy, drying up; flowers stood lined up obediently in flower beds, obedient and tired flowers, just barely able to manage a fragrance, exhausted and exhausting, it was as if in each blossom a tiny empty perfume bottle lay hidden, and under the all-too lush shrubbery there strolled Agnes Deutsch, age twelve, maybe thirteen. Her light brown hair quivered at the back of her head. She wore so-called corkscrew curls. The air smelled of rancid nuts and wrinkled oranges, and Mother slowly crossed the street, with dignity she strode across the chocolate-colored asphalt of the walk that had just been hosed off, past a wrought-iron fence and past the round music pavilion where the musicians were already seated, tuning their instruments, and a sheet of paper lay on a brass table that was made to look like a music stand, carefully inscribed in India ink with the legend: Memories of Herkulesbad.

So Agnes Deutsch, blue-eyed, perhaps a bit cross-eyed, at any rate with a constantly surprised look on her face, not childishly surprised but outraged, eager and ecstatic, Agnes Deutsch, with her hysterical look and her corkscrew curls, walked along the same chocolate-colored sidewalk Mother had walked on, slowly, as though bored—but if bored why that look?—she walked to the outdoor café where a Mrs. Deutsch, Agnes' mother, as I knew, sat at a table in the company of several heavy-legged, gold-bedecked ladies, it was hard to believe, Mrs. Deutsch had blue eyes too but in a face that looked as if someone had just slapped a plateful of cream of wheat on it. Mother knew Mrs. Deutsch, the two greeted one another, and all I had to do was ask Mother if I couldn't look after Agnes Deutsch for a bit, out of politeness and just because a child needs companionship, but I didn't ask, I was as if paralyzed, I hardly dared to look at the hollows of Agnes Deutsch's knees which opened and closed a little at every step, like the hollows of your knees, Miss Moravec, I don't need to describe it further, all you have to do is stand between two mirrors and pretend that you are walking, and then look in the mirror in front of you and in the other mirror observe the angle where the thigh meets the lower leg, it means nothing to you, you don't count your steps and you don't watch yourself as you walk, thank God, but I was twelve years old at that time, or thirteen, all I had to do is think about a woman, any woman, and my mouth would go dry, and I thought about nothing else but women, and out of this dry mouth I gulped down the lust into myself with a dry tongue, a thousand times every day, it's ridiculous, today I'm twenty-two, it's a joke today, and I ought to have more important things to do than to think about hollows of knees or the hollows of Agnes Deutsch's knees, because by now I know what they are: the hollows of knees; bones, flesh, cartilage, muscles, lymph glands, blood vessels, skin. Men have hollows of knees too, the hollows of dead men's knees, as long as the cadavers are still fresh, are no different than the hollows of young and living girls who in Thennberg run to a neighbor to get milk or stroll through the park in Abbazia, slowly so as to prolong the moment a little before having to sit down politely at the outdoor café table next to ladies with cream-of-wheat faces. The hollows of your knees, Miss Moravec, are no different than the hollows of crazy Adalbert Friedländer's knees. I wouldn't have wanted to take him along, but to you I want to show everything, for you I am dunking everything in thick, gray pharmacy-schnapps. My mother's long silk shawl is not here, if it were here you wouldn't be freezing, and I wouldn't be freezing either, but here we are, freezing, warming ourselves in the chill, each warming himself in the other one's chill. The stairs lead to the attic, a spiral staircase without a window. A brown door, a brass door handle. Behind that is the hall with gray wallpaper, two narrow white doors, the shower behind one, the toilet behind the other, another white door opposite, also closed, a small parlor behind it, another door, and then the bedroom. Dampness in the thin walls, lamp shades as if made of bat wings. Yellowish bed linen under the coverlet printed with large yellow flowers. Comb and brush in front of the mirror, reddish-blond hair between the teeth of the comb, perhaps silvery. A wall clock that isn't ticking. Spider webs at the window. On the night table a book: Ulrike Woytich, by Jakob Wassermann. A portrait of Joseph II in a narrow oval frame, a steel-engraving. In the top drawer of the dresser a dark brown, almost black silk stocking. In the shower an egg-shaped cake of soap.

Let's be merry, let's be gay, nothing worse than death can happen to anyone, and if Joachim Schwarzer from Constance, or his successor, or his predecessor, didn't wreck Aunt Paula's apartment: so what? Better than nothing, Phoebus Silbermann would have said. Richard Kranz laughed, but without a sound. Christ died for all of us, he said. Then he said: Nonsense. He heard his own voice. Then he felt like laughing again. He grinned, there was no sound. Miss Moravec was no longer present. Before he left, Richard Kranz thought: Aunt Paula's hair in the comb, sure, why not?

One winter's evening, Judge Mohaupt, speaking to his daughter-in-law:

We have no other choice but to live. To live means, essentially, to distinguish: To distinguish, firstly, between the interests of the individual and the essence of the individual. The interests lead us outward, seduce us, cause us to lose ourselves in the world, dissolve us, extinguish us. With time our interests become more powerful than we ourselves. They become fixed ideas that we follow, even long after they have long ceased to be relevant to our egoism. The more staunchly we hang onto our interests, the more frivolously do we relinquish our own selves.

The essence of the individual, the recognition of this essence, leads inward, makes us immune to seduction, seduces the world to accompany us on our inward journey, to flow into us, to fill us. To be able to travel inward we must recognize the sign that marks our fate. Our fate is the visible manifestation of our character. We must recognize the law of that character, the law of its nature, of its role, of its place in relation to other people. We must act according to that law, even when we may not like it.

The way inward leads not only to a recognition of one's own law, it also leads to a community with all those who have taken the same path. This community is timeless. I, for example, have been able in this way to form intimate friendships with Montaigne and with Lichtenberg. To our Western culture their genius is strangely Oriental. They influence by foregoing any expectation of being able to influence. A landscape is not formed by buildings but by rocks.

As a judge I was, of course, bound to laws, and the process of legislation consists mainly of haggling. The end result of that haggling is preserved in the form of paragraphs, and this by people who have taken the outward path. They had intended to have some influence. This they did, but only for an instant. The outward path leads to nothing permanent. That is why all paragraphs are obsolete the moment they are promulgated.

I attempted to judge according to my own law, and each time I asked myself how the disturbed equilibrium of the world could be restored by my judgment. I sought a balance between the paragraphs and the knowledge of that larger balance. Until the year thirty-four I did not find it difficult to achieve that balance. After the Anschluss it would hardly have been possible for me to accomplish it, but I was already retired by then.

Dictatorships are leaky ships in which things aren't upside down but everything is awry. Only oblique lines are seen as horizontal. All horizontal lines are seen as oblique. The disturbed equilibrium becomes the norm, the disturbance represents the normal condition. One could ask, of course: Is there not a kind of dictatorship at work all the time? Any attempt at an answer on principle would be sheer speculation. It would be a foolish game as well. There is only an empirical answer, and it is statistical in nature. A dictatorship can be recognized by the fact that—for irrational reasons which, however, usually appear exceedingly rational—it will kill not three but thirty people, send to prison not thirty but three hundred, deliberately destroy not three hundred but three thousand, make not three thousand but thirty thousand people miserable, force not thirty thousand but three hundred thousand people to be untrue to themselves, drive not three hundred thousand but three million people to insanity by making them feel that their malaise is not the result of the disturbed equilibrium but a sign of immaturity.

Every dictatorship begins as a dictatorship of the soul over the body, therefore, as a forcible severance of the soul from the body, therefore, after a somersault, finally as conquest of the body, the corporeal over the spirit, over the spiritual, since in this world, because of its material nature, the material is more influential than the spiritual. Whoever separates the material from the spiritual increases the power of the former ten-fold.

And so we must distinguish, secondly, between body and soul. This sounds old-fashioned but is merely a practical simplification. The soul is our will, the body our existence. Our Church considers this existence as something temporary, even something debasing. By the consecration of baptism the Church obligates us to suffer with patience the condition of our corporeality, to overcome by the force of will our susceptibility to the fiendish. In this requirement our Church is not different from a dictatorship. I, however, am not concerned with the Church, I am concerned with life.

If we distinguish between soul and body, not in the sense of our Church but in the sense of life, then the soul makes it possible for us to grasp the chaos that our body resides in, and the body becomes a dependable measure of our phantasies. We will attempt to find a central point between chaos and inner calm, between facts and ideas, between sensuality and self-discipline, here and now, without having to hope for a hereafter. Not dogged strife for the right to go to heaven, only an ever-alert awareness of and never-flagging demand for harmony between spirit and flesh will open the way to timelessness for us—even if this simply means influence upon things and persons which continues, endlessly, for untold generations.

The secret is: hard-wrought harmony. Or disharmony, fought-for in hopes of a consonance that must occur in order to change the disharmony into a new kind of harmony. Only when there is illness does the possibility of recuperation present itself. Destruction, after all, is the surest way for starting the rebuilding process; the building process, in turn, results in destruction, for it offers the appropriate material.

Since, however, attack and defense, destruction and rebuilding, instinct and cognition, soul and body, Christianity and paganism (or better: non-Christian theism), volatility and stability, passion and resignation, house and rocks, do not only exclude each other but also complement each other, even of necessity bring each other about, we must distinguish, thirdly, between ties to these opposites and freedom from them.

But this freedom is only relative, only fleeting, perhaps it is no more than an illusion since we are only humans. We would have to die while still alive in order to free ourselves from all those combative twins. Such a deathlike condition in life is absolutely imaginable, perhaps it is even really possible. And so, what is it we want? A game or death? Are we capable of wanting death? Or is such a decision, to disregard the rules of the game, to see through the game and to hold it in contempt, to interrupt the game for our own self—is this decision not just an extreme way of continuing the game? Is the disregard of the rules of the game not a radical expansion of the game, playfully decided?

Sometimes I like to talk, it gives me pleasure that I still have a voice and that you have ears. Go to bed. If you had earlids as well as eyelids, they would have snapped shut on your ear canals long ago.

I told you a thousand times to put your slippers on when you get up, said Heinrich Moravec to Liselotte Moravec in the kitchen at six o'clock in the morning, here you are standing barefoot on the stone floor, you're bound to catch cold, and then who's going to end up having to nurse you? I told you a thousand times, use the blue towel on your face and the green towel below, after all, a person wouldn't want to wipe their behind and their mouth on the same towel, right? I told you a thousand times to close the window when you're standing around like this, with nothing on, a young girl like you, don't you have any shame at all? You know how people are, all we need is somebody walking by, somebody looking in, somebody seeing you like this, you and me, do you understand?

From the pocket of his gray robe he took a half-empty pack of mold-speckled Junos, put a cigarette in his mouth and lit it.

You're scared, said Lilo. She had tossed her nightgown on the chair and stood in front of the washstand, naked and not quite all naked but from the navel up enveloped in the steam that was rising from the almost boiling water in the wash basin. Scared is what you are, said Lilo once more, bored and just a little spitefully, bending down for the tin can with the cold water (her legs tightened, the curve of her spine, the row of her ribs, the muscles of her boyishly angular buttocks strained against her skin) she raised the can high, let the stream of cold water splash down into the basin, observing with her head to one side the cloud of steam with the thin stream of cold water in the middle that looked like a saber. You're scared, she said a third time into the splashing water, not loudly and not softly, and Heinrich Moravec kept on pretending that he had heard nothing except the splashing of the water, that he was just there, the conscientious father, to supervise his daughter's morning ablutions. In this very spot he had stood three or four weeks after the death of his wife, leaning on his cane, Lilo had been only thirteen then, he had walked into the kitchen early in the morning to get a box of matches from the kitchen cabinet, he had smoked a lot then, right after Helen's death, the first cigarette right after getting up, almost half asleep still, and then fifteen or more during the day (Romanian cigarettes available in any quantity from young Baron Ammer's lawyer), and as he inhaled the smoke that burned his throat and took up his cane again to return to the spare room where he had been spending his nights since the funeral, his glance had accidentally fallen on the other door. Accidentally, or because of the barely audible noise, it sounded like a sigh. The door led to the good room, the parlor as they called it, where Lilo slept, an unlocked door, not quite closed, through the narrow opening one could see the warmth of the sleep-laden darkness, could hear halting breath. Into this darkness he had entered, with fatherly concern, had crushed the cigarette in the ashtray, slowly and circumspectly, had placed the cane, slowly and circum-

circumspectly, against the chair on which lay the girl's dress, black, a mourning dress; then he had stood before the sofa, to listen to this halting, convulsive, sick breathing and to leave again, and yet not to leave but to bend over the sleeping girl in fatherly love; she had not been asleep, had lain there with her eyes open, weeping, not hard, not with a lot of tears as a thirteen-year old child would weep, she had wept with dry eyes.

So he had bent down, Lilo, he had said, what's the matter, come now, it's terrible, I know, terrible, he had said, softly, he had wanted to whisper but the nicotine smoke had lain on his vocal chords, his voice had sounded hoarse, come, Lilo, it's terrible, the hoarse voice had said, come now, be still now, look. He had sat on the edge of the sofa then, helpless and anxious, the left hand on the thigh of his shorter leg, the right on the sheet, three, then two and then only one finger-width away from the edge of the blanket, Lilo, he had whispered, his voice cracking, come now, Lilo, look; he had put his right hand on her forehead, it was not feverish, thank God, he had stroked her forehead and her hair and her face; don't cry, we'll never forget Mommy; his fingers had slid over her face, over her eyelids which had closed under his touch, over her lips. They had tightened, relaxed, tightened again, there was a strange sound, perhaps Lilo had kissed the hand that lay on her face. Come now, don't be so sad, he had sad in a fatherly whisper, come on, don't cry, go ahead and cry, cry yourself out, Mommy is in heaven, go ahead and cry, come, I'll comfort you—he had wanted to say I'll comfort you but something forbade him to say these few words, he had been silent but he had continued to speak soundlessly, to himself, to Helen, the dead one, he had soundlessly said, Helen, little golden dove, Helen, I'll comfort you. He had been sitting upright still, his hand had brushed across her neck, had come to rest on one shoulder and then had returned to the neck, it was a slender, defenseless neck, much too thin to fill the arc between thumb and index finger, the neck of a child. Helen, the voice had said soundlessly, Helen. Suddenly a sob had burst from his chest, a weeping, it had shaken his shoulders, had forced tears into his eyes; he had not wept at Helen's death-bed, nor at her open grave, now he was overcome by weeping, at last, and because he had been so completely surprised by his grief, had so completely surrendered to his sobbing, because he had at last given up his leaden self-control, so the calm, paternally loving fingers had slipped from his control as well, fingers of one afflicted, they had slid down to a waist, just a waist, had nestled against the bud of a girl's breast, his body, until then painfully supported by the shorter left leg, finally liberated from its rigor by the eruption of pain, his body had dropped onto the sofa next to the other body. No, a voice had cried out, some young girl's voice, no; the other body had pushed against the arms, much too violently, much too weakly; don't beat me, the voice had cried out, don't beat me, not with the cane, a young girl's voice, shrill and unfamiliar, no, not my neck; then that other body had lain tightly between his two arms, motionless, helpless, and those pain-curved, now liberated fingers had escaped to the genital cleft, had been received in a womb, a mother's womb, and that halting, convulsive breathing started again, became more agitated, died down. See, he had wanted to say but something had choked the words back into his throat, see, I'll comfort you, I comforted you, come, be still now and sleep. Her breath had come more slowly but her breathing was still loud, too loud, and so she wouldn't have to breathe so loud, so she would go to sleep at last, quietly, a comforted child, he had touched her half-open mouth with his lips, only for an instant, it had been a good-night kiss. A good-morning kiss; already it was light, he had closed his eyes, and it seemed to him that through his closed lids he could see Helen. She was no longer dead, she had risen from the dead, had softly entered the room and stopped in front of the sofa, she had smiled and he had said to her: Our child, I comforted our child; and then, bye and bye, he had gone to sleep in pleasant warmth, unsatisfied, next to the girl whom he had satisfied, comforted and satisfied, she lay there as if dead, freed from pain, he had done a good deed. When a few days later he brought her into his bed she didn't think of screaming. Nor did he ever beat her again after that.

Now he stood once more in the same spot in the kitchen, smoking his cigarette, listening to the splashing of the water, hearing what she was saying and pretending that he didn't hear it. Scared, that's what you are, said Lilo, you begged, you cursed, you implored, you threatened, you went down on your knees, you wanted to beat me, but now, now you don't have the nerve; since young Kranz is in the house you don't have the nerve.

She picked up the soap, straightened up, raised her left arm to pass the cake of soap across the underarm, washed her left arm, then put the soap down and scrubbed her neck with both hands, it looked as if she was trying to strangle herself. Strangle, Heinrich Moravec said soundlessly, and aloud he said: Never mind, just hurry up, will you. Then Lilo had disappeared from the cloud of steam, only her voice had come back to the kitchen. You're afraid of young Kranz, the voice said, don't pull a face like you swallowed a mouthful of vinegar, I was just talking.

Just talking, babbling nonsense, she's gone off her rocker, Heinrich Moravec said aloud. He had walked out of the house, without purpose at first but then not at all without purpose; he stood in the church.

Reverend Horowitz was busying himself before the altar, wearily, slowly, silently, he genuflected heavily, leaning on crazy Ambrose's arm, then he raised himself up again, bowed before the tabernacle, turned around, opened his arms briefly, turned his back to the nave of the church once more, said something, maybe a Latin word, maybe something else; maybe while celebrating Mass Reverend Horowitz carried on a conversation with crazy Ambrose who played the part of altar boy; it seemed as though in the empty church Reverend Horowitz and crazy Ambrose were performing a dance before the Blessed Sacrament.

Heinrich Moravec waited. No, not to the confessional, Reverend Horowitz said later, my God, these confessionals, hard, dark, and the grating, a symbol, but I know all the faces anyway, I see them even when I can't see them, so what's the point of the grating, Reverend Horowitz said, come, my son, we'll be nice and quiet in the sacristy, sit down, my son, speak, my son, you are still living in a state of mortal sin, aren't you? Heinrich Moravec said: She's going to leave me, she's going to give me away, they'll lock me up, they'll ridicule her, what can I do? She's gone off her rocker, Heinrich Moravec said, babbling nonsense, maybe young Kranz was awake, sitting up there in the bedroom, listening, maybe he heard everything, she'll spill everything, maybe she's already done it, to get rid of Moravec, old man Moravec, or maybe just to annoy him, or to brag about it. Old man Moravec, she won't just leave him, first she'll denounce him, drag him into court, into jail, that little whore, insatiable. (Reverend Horowitz said: Now, now, my son.) Here we are, the first time a young man comes into the house, the first time she sleeps under the same roof with a young man she goes crazy, crazy for him, crazy for anyone who'll put his hand between her legs—and I love her, but what's the use, what good is it to her, anyone is better as long as he's younger than Moravec, even this milksop is better, this good-for-nothing, this degenerate. I want to marry her, why am I not allowed to marry her? It would all be so simple if I could marry her; we are living as man and wife right now; if I could marry her it wouldn't be a sin anymore, it wouldn't be dangerous any more, please, Reverend, have faith in us. (Are you finished? Reverend Horowitz asked softly, whisperingly—he was old—resting the wrinkled head in his hand, are you finished? Well then: She is fifteen, isn't she? She is your daughter, isn't she? You have led her into sin, have you not? Something awful is going to happen, said Heinrich Moravec.

He left. On the street Katherina Mohaupt came toward him. He greeted her. Once home he hobbled down to the cellar, closed the door behind him, put the small case on the table, snapped it open and took the short, sturdy pistol in his hand. It was a Russian make, a Soviet army pistol. A comrade of Vitus Wallach's, a taciturn bachelor by the name of Manfred Taub, who later was listed as missing on the Eastern front, had captured it somewhere near Minsk, together with the proper ammunition. On his last leave in nineteen hundred forty-four he had sold it to old Baron Ammer for a small keg of cherry brandy. Baron Ammer had bequeathed it, so to speak, to Heinrich Moravec, or rather, had personally handed it to Heinrich Moravec three weeks before his passing, under four eyes as was proper: without a permit the baron had no business owning a weapon even in his will. (Officially Heinrich Moravec inherited all the antlers and all the stuffed bustards and pheasants with which old Ammer had decorated his hunting lodge on the Eichelberg, impressive specimens, one of them, the antlers of a fabulous stag, had been mounted over the front door of Heinrich Moravec's house.) At the time, the baron had told how Manfred Taub had looked him up in February of forty-three and had asked him if he wouldn't be interested in a weapon that could be had very cheaply, for a ridiculous amount, or else for something to drink, a Russian army pistol with ammunition, small, easy to hide, easy to find too, as it turned out, the previous owner of the pistol, a teacher from Minsk, a World War I invalid by the way, had kept it carefully hidden in the cellar at the bottom of a basket full of old papers, but it was found during a house search, and the teacher—Manfred Taub—hadn't said anything more, so the baron said, but had put his hand around his neck indicating that the teacher had been hanged. It will be safer with you, the baron had told Moravec, I don't want them to find it in my apartment after I—, and he had grabbed himself by the throat as Manfred Taub had grabbed himself by the throat. Not that I'll get hanged, I guess, he had added, but none of us are going to live forever, and you, Herr Moravec, have always had an interest in weapons, you'll forgive me if I put it this way:

Anyone who must walk with a limp would like to own a weapon; you've always been a kind of weapon fanatic, a weapon fetishist, you can use something like this, think of it, Herr Moravec, as if you have been given an iron watchdog, a metal bulldog, you have a young girl in the house, after all, and you too, the baron had said, you'll be able to make use of a watchdog, that's for sure, Herr Moravec, you'll be around for a long time, one can tell just by looking at you, you have high aspirations, that's written all over your face, if you'll pardon the personal remark, and people who have high aspirations need a dependable watchdog, on the other hand if I should be mistaken and you don't have high aspirations but far higher aspirations, five stories higher, the baron had said, in other words, if you want to kill yourself, well then you'll at least have a dependable tool in hand.

You'll get the trophies too, all the hunting trophies, I think that goes with a pistol, stuffed bodies and bones of dead animals belong with a pistol. It makes me happy, the baron had said, that I can bequeath death to you when I'm already, so to speak, in touch with death, so that you can, in turn, bequeath it to the person of your choice. Moravec had thanked him, had taken the package home and had put the small, flat case in the cellar. He had held the pistol in his hand many times since then, had always put it in his pocket when going into the woods for firewood, against governmental regulations, old and new, anything is liable to happen to you in the woods. The body of innkeeper Stanzl lay in the woods, just three weeks ago, he'd been beaten up and robbed, then strangled. A dead man lay in the woods, nobody knew him, he'd been killed with an axe, just three days ago the body of crazy Gretl Viebck had lain in the woods, that idiot girl, raped, shot to death, men roamed the woods, C-campers on the way home, illegal aliens, Russian military personnel, Nazis on the run, soldiers in uniform and deserters in stolen boots and coats, murder was rampant in the woods, what difference if somewhere in the underbrush there lay a forth body, or a fifth?

Heinrich Moravec went back upstairs, threw his fur jacket around his shoulders and limped out into the street again so as not to see Lilo or Richard Kranz, he went for a walk, again without purpose and then not without purpose but toward the manor house that belonged to young Ammer, or maybe to young Kranz: if his parents were actually no longer living he'd be the sole beneficiary, and if the old baron had sold the manor house to Ferdinand Kranz, he'd be inheriting the manor house too; one will have to clarify the ownership situation, clarify it and bring order into it. The sunlight was beginning to carry some warmth, and propelled by that warmth and finally carried by it, Heinrich Moravec reached the manor house. A rocking chair stood in front of the entrance. Clarify and bring order, order and clarify, Heinrich Moravec sat rocking, floating under the plane trees, surveying what had to be done, hovering over the manor house roof, as all the while his right foot kept beating the dust to keep the rocking chair going, and his left leg swung this way and that way, dangling in the air.

Four young Russians rode through the village on small horses, wiry young fellows, their machine pistols hanging aslant on their backs as if they were musical instruments (that was their anxiously affectionate nickname too: Dawaj-guitars). From his rocking chair Heinrich Moravec followed the four horsemen with his eyes, letting his left foot dangle this way and that, someone was maybe dangling on a rope in the woods, not he, Heinrich Moravec, not yet, nothing had happened to him yet, he had not done anything yet, no, not yet. Katherina Mohaupt observed the four horsemen through the open door of the pharmacy, maybe one of them had shot Erich Mohaupt dead, maybe one of them had beaten Erich Mohaupt. She saw her husband's face in the air as if it were painted on glass, the face of a dead man. Judge Mohaupt said to her: They won't do anything to you. Every morning he came to sit in the pharmacy. She shook her head and said to herself: The first of them brings pestilence, the second one brings war, the third of them brings famine and the fourth of them brings death. Judge Mohaupt said: Four young people riding through a village, it is not their village, a strange village named Thennberg is just a bunch of houses to them, that's all, in Russia the villages are different, shall I tell you about Russian villages? Katherina Mohaupt just shook her head. Liselotte Moravec, at home in the kitchen making herb tea, heard the beating of the hooves, she wanted to call out, to get the C-camper Richard Kranz from the bedroom, hadn't he been taken in to protect the house, but she didn't call out, somehow her throat got all tied up. She ran to the door and locked it. Richard Kranz, asleep in Heinrich Moravec's bedroom, woke up, went to the window and saw the four little Russians, he didn't see them clearly, his eyes hadn't thawed out yet, they were still like chilled, shrunken pieces of ice. For the last two or three years, if he managed to go to sleep at all he would wake up with dead eyes, practically blind, it took fifteen minutes before he could see clearly. Maybe it was just a vitamin deficiency.

It would take fifteen minutes, so he went to lie down again on the bed on which he had lain then, on Helen Wallach's body, he closed his eyes, there was a noise, somewhere in the house some piece of metal had dropped to the floor, maybe the lid from a pot, maybe in the kitchen, maybe Liselotte Moravec was in the kitchen, her father called her Lilo.

What good will it do, thought Richard Kranz as he pushed the heavy feather-bed away from his body, why go downstairs to her, from Helen's bed to Lilo's table, what should I say to her, why in the world should I say anything to her, thought Richard Kranz as he washed his hands and face in the cold water, why do I want her to care about me or to like me or to love me, do I care about her, do I like her, do I love her, Richard Kranz thought as he slipped into the shirt and trousers Heinrich Moravec had given him, why am I here, in this particular house, in this particular village, what am I doing here, what are all the others doing here, why did they all just want the one thing, to be cared about, to be liked, to be loved? Why did they all lie so doggedly for the sake of that love, thought Richard Kranz as he laced up his heavy shoes, their soles laden with the water they had soaked up, why did Grandpa Kranz and Grandfather Rombach and their wives, and Mother and Dad too, why would they want to pretend that they had rearranged the preferences of this village, of this country, of the world, why did they all take part in this life-and-death theater, cheerfully entering into the embarrassment of this game, why didn't they want to just be themselves, nor even like the other people but like lap dogs, or guard-dogs,or bloodhounds for the others? Suddenly Grandfather Rombach stood before Richard Kranz as though pasted on the dark inside of his eyelids, short, fat, his head angular like a cube-shaped piece of lead, a little tuft of hair between his short upper lip and his broad, flat nose—the nose of a Babylonian slave—like Charlie Chaplin, like Adolf Hitler, the short, beefy arms and the hairy little hands raised high, in a blessing, in a curse, gesticulating.

Lilo looked at him. You sure slept a long time, Herr Kranz she said, but I saved some tea for you, Herr Kranz, sit down at the table, have some tea, we have bread and lard too if you eat that sort of thing. Thank you, said Richard Kranz. Because I understand, Lilo said, that Jews are forbidden to eat pork or lard made from pork. I am not a Jew, said Richard Kranz. Aren't you funny, though, Lilo said, if you're not a Jew how can you protect us from the Russians? Heinz says it's better to have a Jew in the house who's just out of C-camp, did you at least really come out of C-camp? Yes, said Richard Kranz. All right, so drink your tea and eat your bread and lard. You sure look like a scarecrow, are you sick? I would like to go to the cemetery, said Richard Kranz, if you have nothing better to do you could come with me, because I have forgotten where the cemetery is. To the cemetery? Lilo asked. I heard that an old acquaintance of mine has died, said Richard Kranz, her name was Helen Wallach, I would like to visit her grave. Why? Lilo's question came out of the thick steam over the tea kettle. Nothing special, said Richard Kranz. There are Russians around, Lilo said, it's better not to leave the house when there are Russians around. Nobody will hurt you if you're with me, said Richard Kranz.

Fat little Jakob Rombach floated in the air. The street was deserted. He flew along like a chubby bat. My father's father was Maximilian Kranz, his wife's name was Fanny, said Richard Kranz. My mother's father was Jakob Rombach and his wife's name was Hermione. What about it? Lilo asked. Just talking, said Richard Kranz. Oh, Lilo said, I guess we've got time until the cemetery. It won't do any harm for you to get to know me a little better, said Richard Kranz, it might come in handy. Why? Lilo asked. Because you are beautiful, said Richard Kranz. More beautiful than my mother? Lilo asked.

Jakob Rombach wore a tuft of hair between his Babylonian slave's nose and his too-short upper lip, said Richard Kranz, or he just thought it. He talked incessantly and thought incessantly, his thoughts came faster than words, so he must have thought some of it out loud and some of it without words, he didn't hear his voice, maybe this mix-up was the result of a vitamin deficiency too. Jakob Rombach had grown this mustache, said, or only thought Richard Kranz, in order to look older than he really was (so Mother had said), for as a young man he had wanted to marry the proprietor of a knitwear store, an elderly widow, "big as a hippopotamus," but the widow had married an innkeeper because he, like her first husband, played tarots with a group of better gentlemen, and Jakob Rombach much later took the daughter of a mirror manufacturer to wife, her name was Hermione and she didn't live very long. He was many years older than his wife, but he kept the mustache anyway, because he thought that the mustache made his soft, square face look more brutal and more ordinary. Jakob Rombach had the fixed idea (so Mother had said) that he was much too soft for this life, and therefore he had to pretend to be ruthless. And so he was actually considered to be a common and brutal man, even his daughters thought he was "uncouth"; when he came to the nursery in the evening they would hide their faces in the pillow because they didn't want a good-night kiss, they said his mustache was scratchy and prickly and smelled of tobacco and left-over food. By a hair their mother's and father's marriage had foundered on this mustache. After Grandma Fanny Kranz, Father's mother, already a widow by then, had seen Jakob Rombach, her son's future father-in-law, "she announced decisively" (so Mother said), that she would never let her son marry the daughter of this peasant. Fanny Kranz was very refined. Her father had been an estate manager in Batschka, and on the side he had traded in flour and other victuals. Her erstwhile husband, Maximilian Kranz, had been very refined too. He had owned a print shop, and many aristocrats had been among his clientele. Even the parents of the unfortunate Mary Vetsera had their visiting cards printed by Maximilian Kranz. But Grandpapa died relatively young, because of all that refinement (so Mother said), what happened was that he fell off his horse on the main boulevard of the Prater and broke his neck, "what's a proprietor of a printing press doing sitting on a horse?" After that Fanny Kranz managed the printing press by herself, because her sons, Ferdinand and Eduard, were even much more refined than she and didn't want to have anything to do with the press. Grandma almost made it to Lady of the Star-Cross. She sold the press and retired to private life after her father, the estate manager who survived her husband, had been elevated to the rank of baron owing to his creditable dealings in flour and victuals, but even so Grandma didn't get accepted into the order, and so she bequeathed a portion of her estate to the Ursuline nuns, so at least her remains could be those of a well-born and Catholic lady. What she couldn't achieve in her lifetime (so Mother said) she achieved in her death: she is buried right behind the high altar, at the wall of the chapel of the Ursulines, and the porphyry cross on her sepulchre doesn't just say "Frau Fanny Kranz," but in addition "one Baroness Kronfeld,

Industrialist's widow." If Jakob Rombach hadn't thought that he had to play the ruffian and simpleton, he would have got along very well with his son-in-law's mother. He might even have married his in-law in his old age, and the two oldsters might have been happy together, or at least less unhappy than they ended up being in their loneliness. Secretly Jakob Rombach had a refined soul. After his death (so Mother said) they found a notebook in the drawer of his night table where he had written in large, coarse letters notes like "you work yourself to death, but what for, in heaven's name, what for?" Or "The noblest nation is resignation (Nestroy)" or "And whenever I happen to feel like going for a walk, the sun doesn't shine, and when the sun shines I just don't feel like going for a walk."

And Father played a game too, he played Ferdinand Kranz, bank director; he would have wanted to spend every day when the light began to fade sitting in a house of palms drinking a glass of port, looking out at an autumnal park with peacocks strutting about. He liked to talk about wagon-lits and about suites and about soirees, and since he enjoyed the sound of these and similar words he traveled much and often stayed in first-class hotels and liked to accept invitations to elegant homes, because on the occasion of the travels, the hotels, the invitations, etc., he had the opportunity to enunciate these words over and over, in spite of the fact that what he really would have preferred to do is to stay home by himself, with a cup of tea on the table and a book in his hand. Father always looked as if he were exhausted, he dressed elegantly, his eyes were dark and beautiful, he could never open them all the way because of his exhaustion, his mouth, too, was always half open because of all that exhaustion, this made him look sarcastic, melancholy, resigned, "a delicate, restless mouth" (Mother had said). Aunt Paula, Mother's sister, played the role of a Swiss Lady Milford, always with a round brooch at her wrinkled neck with the photograph of her Italian: the picture showed him in the role of Rigoletto with his mouth wide open. And Mother spent her entire life distancing herself from her father's mustache and from his coarse and brutal appearance. She would always come sweeping up to you, magnificent like a cloud, she was surly, overbearing, eccentric, a woman of the world with the body of a big, over-ripe peach and with the soul of the encapsulated bitter content of a peach stone (that used to be a game: To crack the peach stones with a hammer and to eat the soft insides, they were poisonous and they had a slightly sweet odor), and from this soul there emerged wondrous enthusiasms, in her early years Mother had been filled with unconditional enthusiasm for psychoanalysis, for kinesthetics, for Rudolf Steiner, for Marxism, for African music, she wanted to become a doctor so she could heal people, and heal humanity in the process as well, even later when she was already a woman of the world, she would say things like "love is biology." Uncle Edi, Father's brother, Eduard Kranz of Anglo-Danubia, took on the role of country squire. He played landed gentry, he had thousands of acquaintances, each of them became a hero of his anecdotes, and the way he talked about his anecdotal heroes was as though they had once been buddies in the army, or as though they were his personal property, or quaint but inferior aliens. Don't laugh right away, Baron Ammer, Uncle Edi had said one time (he was sitting at the green table in front of the manor house one evening under the plane trees), have a little patience, Baron Ammer! With me you have to have patience, you know, an awful lot of patience, Constantin Nicolescu already said that, he was a Romanian from Fiume, seafood exports-imports, although he had studied to be a harpist originally, an elegant man, later on he dealt in leather as well and smelled of salt, one could never quite determine whether it was perspiration or the sea air. The ladies didn't mind, they didn't notice the odor or else they liked it, at any rate, good old Nicolescu was some ladies' man. He wore a short beard which he carefully pomaded, he always carried a small pistol with a mother-of-pearl decorated handle, a so-called ladies' pistol—a pistol for shooting ladies only, we thought. He was in great shape, our friend Nicolescu, his uncle owned a tobacco factory in Braila, the daughter of this uncle used to dance at her father's command with a tambourine that had red silk ribbons hanging down to the floor, and she would shake her hair like a gipsy. Life is a puff of air, she would sing, life is a puff from my lips, who will kiss me, who will kiss me? And she would make eyes as if her uncle were standing before her, Constantin Nicolescu in person, a bull's pizzle in his hand, for he could get wild, our good Nicolescu. The room in which the girl danced smelled of honey and mutton and garlic and cinnamon. But even this wild horse with his bull's pizzle once said: Alright, we have to have patience with you, I know. Uncle Edi started to laugh, he laughed alone, he felt it to be his privilege to laugh uproariously without regard to anybody else.

Phoebus Silberman played the busy lawyer even in the concentration camp, Phoebus Silberman from Stanislau, friend to inventors, and Adalbert Friedländer had disguised himself as an SS-man, and in Abbazia Frau Deutsch acted as if her mother had not been a fish monger at the Pressburg market but the ailing daughter of a lord, but Agnes Deutsch didn't play a role, she suffered from the unpredictability of her own moods, she always wanted to be soft but ended up being stiff and harsh, she was sensitive, nervous, delicate, stubborn, she made her corkscrew curls tremble, she let that fraudulent lady who was her mother sit in the outdoor café in Abbazia and stood in front of the music pavilion, her hysterical blue eyes focused on the shoe of an oboe player who was moving his foot up and down to the beat of the music; it was a waltz. My grandparents were visionaries, or else they were collectors of money, but they died honorably; Mother and Father put on a show for people and for themselves as well, and still they were murdered in the gas chambers of Auschwitz and burned in the crematorium (Adalbert Friedländer said he had reliable information about this); Uncle Edi, the gentleman and country squire, was in the concentration camp of Bergen-Belsen for a time, presumably long since dead; maybe Frau Deutsch was still alive, maybe she had died; Adalbert Friedländer was shot to death by a Russian; Phoebus Silberman had cunningly triumphed over cold, hunger, beatings, bedbugs, over the envy of his comrades and the hatred of his enemies, had perhaps even managed to beat his own willingness to die, or perhaps she hadn't; but what became of Agnes Deutsch? Where did that hysterical blue look in her eyes disappear to, in what crematorium did those eyeballs get incinerated?

And Richard Kranz played Richard Kranz. He knew it. And still he played, sensually and obstinately he kept playing, playing the boy of yore who had come back to Helen Wallach, to her daughter whose name was Lilo and who could be Agnes Deutsch, who had come back to his childhood, to his only girlfriend, to the beautiful luxury of longing for the pleasures of the flesh, for self-annihilation through love. Perhaps he owed his life just to this longing. Now this longing crystallized around a central point, became solid, apparent, transparent. Richard Kranz could feel it: this sensual playing with a role, with a mask; and for an instant he understood that all Lilo was to him was an occasion for some sort of dalliance, for a trifling gameøand that's what he needed at last, this playing with the variability of himselføan occasion to find his way back, from the unambiguousness of the threat of death back to cozy ambiguity, to comforting hesitation, day-dreaming and dreamy desires of earlier times. But in the next second Richard Kranz felt only the desire to put his arms around the girl's slight body, to push his tongue between her lips, to penetrate her.

The fact of the matter is, Richard Kranz

thought or said (but this time he heard his own voice), that you have no choice but to go with me into the next bush, no, not to the next bush but straight to Vienna. You're nuts, Lilo said. Or we can go to the manor house, said Richard Kranz. Helen Wallach's grave was one of many, a slight mound of earth, an iron cross, painted black, with a name painted in white on the black metal of the crossbar. "Moravec?" It was odd, a happenstance, like in the theater, trivial. Richard Kranz said: Could be that I am nuts, and furthermore I have very likely lost my so-called good manners in the last few years. There you go, said Lilo. What does that mean: there you go? asked Richard Kranz. I used to admire your mother very much, he said, and on top of that you have eyes like Agnes Deutsch. I will not take you to Vienna but straight to Abbazia, he said. We'll do somersaults there, the sand on the beach is nice and warm. Where is that, Lilo asked?

Your mother—said Richard Kranz. He wasn't able to finish the sentence. A small cloud of dust rose somewhere on the road, two hundred feet from the cemetery. The ground was damp, but where wheels had squeezed the dirt up from the ruts, the dried earth crumbled under hooves. Jesus, the Russians, said Lilo. She jumped up, leapt, flew along the rows of graves, there was a shed by the cemetery wall, the door hinges squealed. How distant all this is, thought Richard Kranz, four young Russians are riding along on little horses, what are they doing riding along, what do I care about them? A girl runs away, so we'll follow her, away from the grave of the loved one on a narrow path to a wooden shed, we follow on knobby legs, soon we'll try to pull the clothes off her body to see her naked, feel her naked—and we've seen five hundred or fifteen hundred naked bodies in these last years, live ones and dead ones, all made from the same boring model, why are we not nauseated, one ought to be nauseated, one ought to be bored and frightened, one ought to be saturated with the stench of cadavers, with body odors, and would you believe it, we go after a girl, we will sniff and paw at her body, and in the end we will lie together someplace and believe we are in love, just because we have sniffed one another, pawed, licked one another, copulated, what's the point of it all? With each step he swayed his head as if in amazement, and there he stood before the low wooden shed, the door-hinges squealed. Spades leaned against the wooden wall, hoes, shovels, boards, rakes, the air smelled of stagnant water, light trickled in through cracks as wide as a finger, it was neither light nor dark, as if the shed were under water; Lilo was leaning against the wall, wrapped up in her heavy coat and kerchiefs.

She raised her arms and said something he didn't understand, he could barely hear her, he laid his hand on her kerchief and felt the curve of her skull, what's the point of all this, he thought as his mouth touched the cool, chapped lips, what's the point of all this? And as he separated the two rows of teeth, running his tongue over the other tongue, he continued to think, distinctly, wonderingly, questioningly, somebody leans against a wooden wall, kissing a girl, why is he kissing her? But at the same time he thought this, another was thinking for him as well, thinking: You've come home, you've come back after all to someplace, home, maybe the orchestra in Abbazia will start playing that waltz, maybe you just dreamed the hunger and the beatings and the bedbugs, maybe it'll be evening soon, Frau Deutsch is sitting at the table of the outdoor café in all the disgusting opulence of her overblown body and her jingling jewelry, and Mother is waiting at home, and the cats are yowling on the manor house roof, and the chain of the well is rattling in Helen Wallach's courtyard.

You don't smell any different, Lilo said later. What do you mean? asked Richard Kranz. I mean, Lilo said, a Jew ought to smell different. I'm not a Jew, said Richard Kranz. Oh, I see, Lilo said. A little later she said: You'll march yourself right on to Vienna now, and don't you dream of saying anything to Heinz. You'll tell him everything yourself, said Richard Kranz, and then he asked: How was that, before? What did you say? And Lilo didn't want to answer, but he kept asking her, so finally she lowered her eyes and, so softly that one could barely hear it, she whispered as if to herself: I said, you poor thing, you poor thing, you poor thing.

Well, I just thought it would be better if you'd hear it from me directly, Heinrich Moravec had told Erich Mohaupt some years later, as alderman you're bound to hear about something like this, and anyway, there's no reason to conceal anything about this business, you as a combat-veteran know only too well that they're just after making a stink, what is it they want with the poor child, everybody knows I was a good father to her, I was downright crazy about her, let the dead rest in peace is what I say, but there are always people to whom nothing is sacred, Doctor Zahidil is the examining magistrate, never heard of him, so he had to serve a summons on me, had to bother with such ridiculous stuff, because of some anonymous tips, or rather, because of a single anonymous tip, because I got too big for them, so they want to give it to Moravec, and with our taxes too, Herr Pharmacist.

Then Heinrich Moravec asked whether the pharmacist didn't happen to know who had informed against him, Erich Mohaupt had shaken his head, and Heinrich Moravec had driven away in his Mercedes with the specially designed clutch pedal to accommodate his shorter left leg. Later, after closing time, Erich Mohaupt had finally taken a seat, in the same corner where his father used to sit, day after day until his death, in the same small leather-covered armchair. I believe, Judge Mohaupt had once said to his daughter-in-law, that more than anything else things strive for true order, for the moment of balance, and in our particular case this means that I shall not exit until after Erich comes back, not because life is so important to me but because life, our life here, has a use for me until then. I didn't want to believe your father, Katherina Mohaupt had told her husband on the day he returned, but he was right, as it turns out, no sooner did we put him in his grave and here you are, maybe he had to die so you could come home, the good Lord likes exchanges. Then she had given careful and detailed account of the condition of the pharmacy, of the last years and the last days of her father-in-law, of all the anxieties and troubles she had endured, for instance, she told how the Russians had spared the pharmacy not only out of "respect for science," as "Father had admonished them in near-fluent Russian," but because after that he had given them a dozen bottles of home-made fruit schnapps "as earnest-money"; she said that Father had hidden this schnapps in the cellar, long before the end of the war, the Russians had still been in southern Hungary then, and at that same time Father had also begun to brush up on his knowledge of the Russian language that he had picked up in prison camp near Tobolsk during and after the First World War, and had begun to memorize the text of the speech that he ended up actually delivering, "to the end Father's memory was like steel," and in the weeks and months that followed Katherina Mohaupt talked freely and volubly about what had happened at the pharmacy, but about all the other things that had happened in the last days of the war and in the first days of peace she said practically nothing.

Mohaupt listened. With disgust he noted that in all these reports and stories the center of interest was always his father or his wife, that everything was always about the pharmacy, about the vegetable garden, about her own risks, her own ingenuity, her cleverness and weakness, as though all that time the rest of the world had not existed, it seemed to him that since the day of their parting his wife's horizon had narrowed shockingly, he thought Katherina had changed into an insignificant little woman who, animal-like, could experience the world only on her own body, finally he even decided he must have idealized his wife in his memory or worse, back when they had first fallen in love, he must have failed to recognize her true nature. Mohaupt did not show his disappointment. This was not hard for him to do since he wanted to doubt his observations and furthermore, since he had always lived as if in a snail's shell, carefully and conscientiously nurturing the mimicry that isolated and at the same time also protected him. Only much later, about two years after his return, did Mohaupt realize that he had doubted his sad observations not out of sentimentality or out of indolence. He had labored under a delusion.

Only now did he understand this. The conversation had once again been about Father who had admonished the Russians "in near perfect Russian to have respect for science," whereupon they actually departed after first pocketing the twelve bottles of fruit schnapps. This time Katherina added the following sentence to the story: Your friend finished the rest of it.

Mohaupt understood. He had already heard about Richard Kranz's stay in Thennberg. But nothing definite was said. He had remained a shadow. Oh yes, somebody said at the pub, Richard Kranz survived, many have survived, and why not, such a young man, so they made him work. Yes, Herr Pharmacist, said another one, young Kranz paid a visit to your wife, didn't you know? He'll be back, that one, said a third one, and spread himself in the manor house. They did not talk about Kranz often; Erich Mohaupt played tennis with him, didn't he, if he wanted to know something, all he had to do was ask.

Mohaupt did not ask. And now Katherina was saying: Your friend finished the rest of it. She did not say his name. Richard Kranz had remained a shadow to her as well, or else she had reason not to say his name. Mohaupt felt: there was caution in this circumscription, anxiety, her finger had touched the core. My friend? he asked.

Never would he forget the short exchange that followed, nor his wife's demeanor, at first so dull and apathetic as always when she was not talking about herself, about Father, about the pharmacy but about any other—to her seemingly unimportant—occurrences in the rest of the world, but then a light had come into her eyes—nervous, feverish, restless as if in flight—but this strange light did not last long, it changed into a cold glare. For a few seconds those eyes held an expression well-known to him: sheer horror.

Your friend finished the rest of it, she had

said. Who, asked Mohaupt? Young Kranz, Katherina said. Richard Kranz, asked Mohaupt? She nodded. But why did Richard Kranz come to Thennberg, he asked? From the C-camp, she said. He survived, he asked? He was here, she said. Of course, right, said Mohaupt, did he stay in our house? She shook her head. Did he stay at the manor house? asked Mohaupt. At the Moravecs, said Katherina. How come at the Moravecs? he asked. Moravec happened to run into him and he put him up at his house, she said. He could have stayed at the manor house, said Mohaupt. But he stayed at Moravecs, said Katherina. Why? he asked. Because Moravec wanted to have a Jew in the house in case the Russians or anyone else wanted to break into the house, and anyway—she did not finish the sentence. What do you mean, anyway? asked Mohaupt. She said nothing. Just because he wanted to have a Jew in the house was no reason for Kranz to really stay there, said Mohaupt. Still Katherina said nothing. Let's say he fell in love, she finally said. How do you mean, let's say? asked Mohaupt. This went on for several minutes, he asked reasonable questions and she gave non-answers, she said things like "it doesn't take much for a young man to fall in love, you know" or "maybe it wasn't love at all," and her eyes suddenly glowed feverishly. She gave her husband a horror-stricken look. Then she lowered her eyes and did not raise them again, and Mohaupt stopped asking questions.

The following day he wrote to Richard Kranz, at his old Vienna address on Brunerstrasse. He did not receive a reply. This concerned him, but his concern was displaced and covered over by another, reassuring discovery: he understood that his wife's apparent indifference to what had happened in Thennberg was a symptom of an illness, or a sign of recovery, or at least a condition for her recovery. He now saw that the impressions of those months of first love had not deceived him, that his wife's personality had not undergone a change in the last years but rather—and he might have expected it—as all the people in her environment either croaked or survived, and even how they croaked or survived, had been experienced by her in a much too intensive way, almost feverishly, even ecstatically. The reason for her silence was not indifference but an attempt to ward off new bouts of suffering by not talking (or by babbling about pharmacies or vegetable gardens). Her superficial descriptions of the last days of war and of the first days of peace, her inability to bring events into some temporal sequence, her incoherent apologies when she had forgotten to mention this or that, all the hollow and grandiose turns of phrase that had been foreign to her before and that now suddenly appeared in her speech—things like, the spirit of Ambros "became beclouded," the people's fury "did not manifest itself," old Baron Ammer left Heinrich Moravec "a few little valuables"—her inhibited, ragged, hasty descriptions: all those were nothing but self-defense, a necessity of mental hygiene. Katherina was defending herself against the all too brutal effects that apparently resulted from the utterance of certain past occurrences.

Anything that is put into words, thought

Erich Mohaupt, is infinitely more than the sum total of sounds or a series of words: anything that is put into words is almost reality, even when that has long ceased to exist, and since an utterance is a concentrate, subject only to fantasy and free of the many distracting, deconcentrating, noncommittal elements of reality, therefore a word, an utterance, capable of inflicting pain more severe than the original unformulated, unconcentrated experience. Moreover, he further thought, the relation between reality and its formulation through words is actually a paradox. One might believe that reality is permanent and words are fleeting, and suddenly one grasps that reality, having but a single present, is constantly fading away while its mantle endures as it becomes formulated in people's heads and words. If anything, Katherina's only hope was to withhold words and sentences from her horror, to de-realize past actuality by denying it formulation, and then simply to wait for life, everyday life, with its countless new events, to displace all memory. There are poisons that even the healthiest intelligent organism is unable to eliminate; the only thing that one can attempt to do is to minimize their potency. The therapeutics of psychoanalysis is based on a nice illusion, it pictures the soul as a sack that can be emptied. Remaining silent is probably not healthier but it is more human, and perhaps it is enough to hint at some things without giving them clear and direct formulation. He decided (and he felt satisfied with his decision because he believed the world, and with it his own fate, to be serious business from which one could, should, must draw inferences, even if just for the sheer pleasure in one's punctiliousness), he made the decision never to ask his wife about those agitated days but, if it had to happen at all, to wait patiently for the right occasion that would enable her to speak.

When Heinrich Moravec bought the manor house (not from Kranz, not from young Baron Ammer, nor from the Joachim Schwarzer of Constance who had been the last occupant of the manor house, but from a public real estate company that had apparently obtained the building quite legally from one of the earlier owners after it had been stripped by smaller as well as by private realtors and had generally fallen into disrepair), on a hot summer day, Mohaupt and his wife had gone to a fish restaurant on the Danube after closing. Katherina read every line on the menu two or three times, asked whether this fish wasn't too fat and whether that fish didn't have too many bones, then she said that all fish from the Danube tasted of mud, she said it in a somehow provocative way, hoping Mohaupt would contradict her, and they did, in fact, discuss at length whether Danube fish was really muddified, as it was called, or not, and when the waiter came Mohaupt ordered carp prepared the Serbian way and Katherina asked the waiter whether the establishment had any fish that didn't taste of mud, and when the waiter smiled in confusion and shook his head, she said she wanted wine, half a liter, "if my husband wants to drink along, then bring a whole liter," and after the waiter had left she finally asked: Have you heard? Mohaupt cleaned his spectacles and, with his glasses off, he looked at the blurred picture of a woman's head, the waiter brought the wine, Katherina drank, Mohaupt put his glasses back on and took a sip of wine, it smelled of acid and sulphur. Have you heard? Katherina asked a second time, Sir murderer buys a manor house and God doesn't punish him, God will never punish them, not in this world and not in the next, God likes bartering but when it comes to murderers He looks the other way, He doesn't consider them worthy of punishment. Did Moravec do away with somebody? Mohaupt asked cautiously and softly, but even as he asked the question he thought that it would have been better left unsaid, but since he had now uttered that sentence he placed his hand on his wife's arm in a gesture of helpless apology, a large, bony hand, it rested on the freckled skin in fatherly appeasement. Katherina looked down in amazement at the five bony fingers, as if she had never in her life seen a hand, at least not one that touched her arm, then she raised her head, looked at the lights on the opposite bank and nervously emptied her glass. Her eyes again took on that restlessly feverish look and then became fixed in a seeming totally vacant stare, no longer conscious of the brightly covered restaurant tables, the illuminated tree branches, the people sitting all about them, the perspiring waiters, but quite inner-directed, toward a single point of cerebral matter. It'll pass in five, no in two minutes, Moravec thought to himself, she's still sick, she's got to get a hold of herself, she's got to learn to forget, she's got to get well, she's the only important one, to hell with the rest of them, murderers or not. He took his hand away from her arm, waiting, wanting to comfort her with a short sentence like, "Kathi, what's wrong?" (that's what he used to call her, Kathi, sometimes he still called her that, Kathi had become her secret nocturnal name), or, "Don't take it so hard," or, "Come now, see, I'm right here," but then he decided it would be better not to say anything after all, to leave her alone with an emotion that he could not share with her. Eventually he found a sentence that he thought he could say without exciting her further: Don't you want to eat something after all? She nodded. A waiter passed by, an older man, a little on the heavy side. Mohaupt waved him to the table. With her fixed, horror-stricken eyes Katherina looked into the reddish, puffy, greasily shining face and said: Yes, yes, something to eat, Wiener schnitzel. A salad with it, the waiter asked? Katherina looked at her husband, in astonishment and as though in need of help. Cabbage salad? asked Mohaupt. Cabbage salad, said Katherina. The waiter left. She pulled her mouth into a smile. You should have said coleslaw, she said then, since you've been in the army you only speak High German.

A few days after that Mohaupt went to the cemetery, it was the anniversary of his father's death, no, the anniversary of his mother's death, he wasn't sure, even though, as he tried to convince himself, he was going to the cemetery only to mark the anniversary of his father's or his mother's death with a visit to their shared grave. Maybe it is the anniversary of my future death, he thought as he stood at his parents' grave, before a granite stone engraved with gold letters and numerals that showed the names with the two years under each name but not the birth and death dates. Then he walked past a shed where obviously the gardeners and the grave diggers kept their tools, walked past the chapel and toward the gate, but then he turned away from the gravel-covered path and studied the graves, one after the other, looking for the year 1945, finally found one on the cross of Leopold Stanzl, Mohaupt had known him, "God punishes the wicked," it read, and "Rest in peace!" A child lay next, Ernestine Plzl, born 1943, died 1945, and next to Ernestine Plzl lay some whose name he knew only by hearsay, then a forester's widow Klamm who had a predilection for large dogs (if that stately old woman who had always walked her large dogs was in fact the widow of forester Alois Klamm—as Mohaupt had always thought—and not the widow of the also deceased forester Johann Schober), then a farmer Eckert (a fat old man who often came to the pub, Mohaupt remembered him well), and then a grave, already sunken in, under a wooden cross with a barely legible legend, a Margarethe Viebck (wasn't that the crazy old maid servant?), after her lay many others, and then, on a pink marble stone, "Helen Moravec (1904-1943)" and below that "Liselotte Moravec (1930-1945)" and below that "Heinrich Moravec (1902-)", and all three names were encircled by a single gold flower garland so that no fourth name could be engraved in the stone.

Mohaupt remembered Wallach, the postal clerk and his wife who had later married Heinrich Moravec, Liselotte Moravec was obviously her daughter, a wild, whitish-blonde child, so Moravec had adopted her, and had put his name under the names of his wife and his adoptive daughter, maybe for reasons of economy as some people do, maybe out of piety, because there are people, mostly old ones, who in their lifetime have their names placed on the gravestones below the name of their husband or wife, because they mistrust their heirs, or because every time they visit the cemetery it makes them feel good to prolong the matrimonial union at least by way of a common cemetery address, or maybe Heinrich Moravec chose to formulate his mourning through the inscription by indicating his desire to follow his wife and his adoptive daughter to the grave. The bare spot after the numerals "1902-" was a challenge and, at the same time, a sign of resignation. Until now Mohaupt had never given a thought to where he wanted to be buried, in his parents' grave, or in the grave of his wife, or in his own grave in which the coffin of his wife would then be included. Such group formation, he now thought, was undoubtedly an archaic custom, an almost animalistic expression of instincts that in the face of death are allowed to be exhibited without restraint, that become even glorified and sanctified. By having his name placed below the other two names while still living Heinrich Moravec may have wanted to communicate not only his grief, but also his desire to lie with his wife and with his adoptive daughter even after death; perhaps he had wanted to immortalize a powerful longing with the help of the pink marble. Mohaupt didn't know Moravec well.

He wouldn't put it past him, he thought, to erect a monument to his appetite.

Mohaupt walked on. At the cemetery wall he found some graves that were obviously properly cared for through the good offices of the parsonage but that had inscriptions such as "Here in God rests a fallen soldier of the German Army," or, "To an unknown soul," or, "A true Christian lies in this grave, dead by an unknown hand, 1945, Christ have mercy on us." As Mohaupt walked home from the cemetery, he thought that he really couldn't have found out anything about Heinrich Moravec's supposed murderous deed by this method, and anyway, all he had wanted to do was to visit his father's or his mother's grave.

Then he wrote to Richard Kranz a second time at Brunerstrasse in Vienna, but again he received no answer. When a few months later he had to go to Vienna to take care of some business at the Pharmacists' Board of the Pharmaceutical Compensation Bureau, he left Spitalgasse after his visit to that office. His train wouldn't leave for three-and-a-half hours. Mohaupt crossed Alserstrasse and walked along Lange Gasse, past the house where he had lived as a prep school student. It was November, delicate snowflakes floated in the air like tiny bright insects, then melted away at about the height of a man's shoulders and disappeared; the wet asphalt shone darkly, the color of cheap chocolate. Mohaupt turned left. He walked past the Parliament and then through the Volksgarten. There, close to the creamery, between two already bare trees stood a fir-tree, not rooted but artificial, hung with pieces of gray bread, "The birds' Christmas tree," as a small tablet announced, and the tree was, in fact, thoroughly occupied by crows. From Michaelerplatz and through the passage between little shops Mohaupt arrived at Habsburgergasse. When he was still in prep school he sometimes stood in this passage, waiting for Richard Kranz as he came out of Brunerstrasse, pudgy and always as if too sleek, a boy who had only one desire: not to be who he was, in other words, not the son of bank director Kranz but perhaps the son of farmer Eckert or of forester Klamm, not pale and nervous and well-read and sweet-toothed but calm, uncultured, coarse and vulgar; ever vulnerable in his erratic mind (which wasn't that at all but merely a way of switching too fast from one subject to another), and yet, because of his polite, over-refined, seemingly noncommittal way of expressing himself he always appeared to be covered by an invisible veneer. Richard Kranz was four years younger, and that was a lot. Mohaupt didn't take him seriously, or rather, considered him too serious; he well understood that his friend had to be so very serious in order to stand up to life and thereby to escape his sleekness, he understood that this seriousness gave Richard Kranz his only possibility to let things come toward him and then (in self-defense) to banish them into the realm of fantasy, but even with this shadow boxing that he performed for honest and honorable reasons, the picture that Richard Kranz had of life still became distorted. As reality was transformed into threatening shadows that with pseudo-might crashed into a likewise pseudo-defense-wall which, of course, managed to withstand them, Richard Kranz's real distress was transformed into harmless comedy. He suffered from this feeling of harmlessness, without being able to find the way into real life where true impulses as well as ruses defy true dangers. Richard Kranz had once said, "You have to let them crucify you in order to prove the truth, but then what's the use of the truth when you end up crucified?" and another time: "Once I'd like to be the Duke of York, because then everybody would think I'm the Duke of York and nobody would know that that's who I am."

The house on Brunerstrasse was intact. Richard Kranz and his parents had lived on the second floor, in rooms that smelled of floor polish and of sweet liqueurs. Mohaupt had never enjoyed coming to this apartment, he didn't like his friend's mother, she had always smiled at him and looked at him kindly out of eyes that glistened like cherries, but the smile and the almost loving glance had felt wrong, put on, dishonest. This obliging dishonesty had been submissive: that was what had bothered Mohaupt the most. Likewise the gentleness of Director Kranz whom he met now and then not only in Thennberg, but also at Brunerstrasse, that lassitude, that perpetual suffering from his own refinement was perceived by Mohaupt as artificial. Humility out of arrogance. A shipping company now had offices on the second floor and a "Dipl.-Eng. Mock" lived behind the door opposite, he wasn't at home, the shipping company whose establishment took up the erstwhile Kranz apartment had an anteroom (this may once have been the room that had separated the rear entry of the Kranz apartment from the servants' quarters) where an old man sat reading the newspaper by the blinding glare of a fluorescent ceiling fixture. Looking up from his newspaper, he looked at the entering Mohaupt as though he were a long-suspected burglar who had now been caught in the act. Mohaupt turned, walked back down the stairs to the street floor, stopped in front of the door to the janitor's apartment but didn't have the courage to knock. He didn't know what it was that had paralyzed his hand; perhaps he didn't knock because he really didn't want to find out what Richard Kranz's new address was. The door opened anyway, a fat woman looked him in the face. Silently she examined him at length through slitted eyes, with a hazy look, vacant, benevolent, unsure, a dreamer's look, perhaps the look of an alcoholic. The woman exuded a slightly acidic odor. Mohaupt asked for the address. Now the woman opened her mouth. Between soft lips a tumescent tongue searched for words. An exhalation of schnapps gushed forth. But the dirty pigs got wasted, the woman said in a soft, whining voice, or might the gentleman be from the police? Mohaupt shook his head. What d'you want from me then, said the woman. She turned slowly and closed the door behind herself. Two times she turned the key in the lock, and Mohaupt thought he heard this noise, the smooth interlocking of oiled pieces of metal, on his return trip every time the train's wheels crossed over the little space between two rails.

Had the friendship with Richard Kranz really been a friendship? he mused on his return journey, with the oppressive feeling that he should have rejected the words dirty pigs, should have scolded and lectured the woman, should have stood up for Richard Kranz. Why hadn't he done it, why hadn't he been able to do it, why hadn't he stayed the night in Vienna and the next morning gone to the Central Registration Office, or to a lawyer, or to a private detective agency, to find or have them find Richard Kranz's new address, and then report the woman to the police for that "dirty pigs." He saw her standing in the crack of the door, and behind her, on the wall of the poorly lit room, he saw the lower quarter of an oil painting in a heavy gold frame, above the gold two strangely elongated feet in bright, pointed shoes, he had seen these feet before somewhere, and as he observed the strange shoes reminiscent of roots, it had been evening, china had rattled, tout comprendre et rien pardonner, a woman's voice had said, it was the voice of Frau Kranz, of course, the feet in the bright, pointed shoes were the feet of a clown, the title of the painting was Pierrot and Pierette, the painting of a Frenchman, Frau Kranz had explained once, it had hung in their parlor. Mohaupt went to the dining car. All of a sudden he couldn't tell whether he had recognized the painting in the janitor's apartment right away after seeing the frame and the two feet, or only just now; and if he had recognized it right away, why had he remained silent, why hadn't he called the woman to account and immediately reported the theft to the police? So, had the friendship with Richard Kranz really been a friendship? On the one hand, undoubtedly. But on the other hand: a friendship does not declare itself as friendship, it exists implicitly. Mohaupt made the decision (and once more he took pleasure in his ability to go beyond his musings and to draw clear and practical conclusions from the facts), to find Richard Kranz's address on his next visit to Vienna, and to take another look at the painting in the janitor's apartment. Somewhat reassured he pushed the empty coffee cup aside and drank the contents of three little bottles of schnapps that dining-car waiters called flacons.

Another year passed in silence. Katherina spoke less and less of those troubled days in the spring of 1945. Moreover, another floor was being added to the pharmacy building. The pharmacy flourished, even the woodcutters sent their wives for medications, sometimes one or the other woodcutter's wife would even send her husband for pills. Katherina lost weight. For a long time Mohaupt failed to notice his wife's weight loss; sometimes, after they went to bed, his hand would stroke the waist of a nineteen-year old, his fingertips remembered that intimate touch of long ago. More than anything else, things strive for true order, Father had said. Snow falls in winter, bees hum in the summer. Katherina, it seemed, had chased away her demons or had conquered them: it amounted to the same thing.

Then Heinrich Moravec drove by the pharmacy, stopped, came in, said a few sentences, said the name of Examining Magistrate Dr. Zahidil, drove on in his Mercedes. Somewhat later, after closing, Mohaupt sat in the small, leather-covered armchair in which his father used to sit, smoked his first and only cigarette of the day and decided to ask his wife whether she had informed against Heinrich Moravec. He couldn't really imagine it, one shouldn't punish evil with evil, he despised anonymous informers, hitting someone in the back, unprepared, out of nowhere; but at the same time he felt something like satisfaction that Katherina at least, if not he himself, had after all acknowledged his never honestly felt friendship to Richard Kranz. But that wasn't so important either. If she really did it, Mohaupt thought, then she is finally well now, then she could do nothing else but this one thing in order to get well, then she had to do it, had a right to do it. He walked over to the apartment. He wanted to ask Katherina, but he did not ask before supper, nor after supper, nor did he ask her later when he lay next to her, stroking her waist with a fatherly soothing hand. Sleep well, he said softly, and he still wanted to ask her and waited for her to wish him a good night, but she didn't say anything, and then he felt her mouth against his chin, the hard touch of her teeth, you, she said into his skin between her teeth, you, and suddenly she lay there, her arms flung open and her legs spread wide apart, and then she threw her arms around his neck, pressed her thighs against his hips, it hurt, her lap rose up, engulfed him, and he knew that he didn't have to ask anything, and then all he knew was that he loved her, and not until much later, when he woke up and saw the dawn through the network of the curtain, did he think: Thank God! Finally, finally.

In his testimony before Examining Magistrate Dr. Zahidil, the building contractor Heinrich Moravec said, among other things:

It is difficult for me to speak about my daughter's last days. That is understandable. There are altogether three reasons why it could not be possible for me to set forth the true course of things.

First, I really loved Liselotte, and when one loves, words are not so easily found. I loved her much more than a father could love his own daughter. To a father his own daughter is a child, a gift of God. The gift is welcome but it is also natural. Strike a flint and you get fire, as the saying goes. Where man and woman are together, children will not be lacking. Besides, most fathers don't want daughters, they want sons. But to me Liselotte was not a gift of God but the gift of my late wife. She brought Liselotte with her into the marriage.

This fact was of no importance to me before the wedding. I was in love with my future wife, and I didn't care whether she had children or not. They were all crazy about my future wife. She did not give the slightest encouragement. That is why, at the time, I could hardly believe that I had a chance with her. She was a very respectable wife, and after Wallach had fallen she lead a withdrawn life. She went shopping, now and then she picked Liselotte up from school, occasionally she called on her late husband's women co-workers at the Post Office. That was all. Perhaps she lived such a withdrawn life only because rumor had it that she and young Kranz had a thing going. That damned piece of gossip poisoned my wife's life. As a widow she had to be doubly careful. A widow is quickly talked about. The first time we were alone her manner was unfriendly. I didn't dare hope. But then she took me after all. I do not know why she did. It may be that she was unable to live by herself. Maybe she didn't want to wait any longer. She needed a mainstay, and the child needed a father. Maybe she needed an impeccable man to get rid of the gossip once and for all, and there weren't many men in those days. Not men my age. Most of them were at the front. She took me because I was there. And I was there because I have a limp. Sometimes a cripple takes precedence.

The child was very wild. At the time people asked me: What do you want to saddle yourself with that for? Helen: yes. She is first rate, they said, but the child is the devil personified. I didn't care at all, although as a small child Liselotte really was pretty nasty. Liselotte, I would say to her, I'll give you two pennies if you'll shut your mouth for an hour. Whereupon she would yell even louder. Once she cut a worm in two with a piece of wood. Liselotte, I said, if you'll be good for an hour you'll get a piece of candy. She climbed trees and ripped her dress to shreds. Once she went after her mother with her fists. It wasn't dangerous, her fists were no bigger than apricots and she hardly reached up to her mother's chest. That's when I gave Liselotte her first slap in the face. It was necessary. My wife said it too: That's when you need a man around. I liked to try the candy and the pennies better. When persuasion didn't work, then I had to discipline her. It didn't hurt her. She never cried. She just looked at me and off she went. When she was really awful she got it in the behind. I would put her over my knee and let her have it. It was just slaps though. She hardly felt it. I never beat her with the cane. Or only once in a while. But never on the head. I really had to force myself to do a thing like that. I can be energetic when necessary, but I am not hot-tempered. And besides, I did love her. I saw in her not a child but Helen's daughter. I saw in her a little lady.

I was brought up to look up to the female gender. My grandmother on my father's side was an imposing woman. As a little boy I thought she was the Virgin Mary in person, so much did I revere her. She looked like the saint's image in Church. My parents had a bad marriage. There were lots of rows. Then my mother would sometimes have a tear-stained face when she came into the kitchen where I did my homework. She would stroke my head. You must never forget that you are a little knight, she would say. Or she would say: You are my little protector. When we went to Mass together she always admonished me: You must be polite to little girls, every little girl is a young lady. That was still in grade school. Our teacher never said the word woman, he would always say: the weaker sex. Sometimes he said: the beautiful sex. Women to me were always like the saints.

When my wife died, Liselotte was thirteen. I had to be mother and father to her in one person.

There was little to eat then, in school everything was at sixes and sevens, we did have the BDM but all they mostly did was festivals, they weren't any real help. Besides, there was a lot to do in the business in forty-three. I spent every free minute at home. I did her homework with Liselotte, I saw to it that she washed properly, I bought her the best clothes. Not that you could get much. I had no other thought but Liselotte. I was downright crazy about her. A lady-friend was out of the question for me, for I had my daughter. I saw her mother in her. I nursed her when she was sick; and when I was under the weather she would take care of the house by herself. Are you going to hang yourself? she asked me a full three weeks after her mother's funeral. She would ask such questions. I answered: But I have you. Then she kissed my hand. As time went by she got much better. Occasionally it could happen that she made some trouble and that I had to discipline her. But that happened less and less often. She understood that she couldn't be rebellious. When she was good we had a good life. She even became attached. She took me into her heart, and I loved her far too much. So it is understandable that it is difficult for me to speak about her last days.

I have said: three reasons. The second: since that time I have distinct blanks in my memory. For example, I no longer know exactly what my father looked like. He was short and thin, his hands were in constant motion even when he had nothing to do. He had quick eyes. But I see him only in outline, almost like a shadow. Once in a while I even let a business opportunity slip. I forget appointments, even when I had noted them down on the calendar. I am not what I used to be.

I know, for instance that on that day I asked Liselotte to go into the woods to pick up firewood. There was still wood in the house but we had to get some new because wood has to dry first. As I said, we needed firewood, not only for heating but for cooking too. But I cannot remember whether we were going to have beans or peas that day, although I ought to remember since beans and peas have to be soaked the night before. And I can no longer remember just why I didn't go to the woods myself. Maybe it was because of young Kranz. He fell ill suddenly. That started the day before. I had gone to the pharmacy right away to get aspirin for him. I did have my connections. Old Mohaupt was sitting in the pharmacy. He worried his head over nothing as old people have a way of doing. He said if young Kranz should die he would have to get a Jewish funeral. I said: How could that be done when there aren't any Jews anywhere around any longer, and besides, young Kranz had been baptized a Catholic. Such details I retain. I remember my daughter's funeral as well. As if it were today I see all the many people at the cemetery, Reverend Horowitz, the fresh flowers—it was already spring—and I also know that I was afraid young Kranz might suddenly stand at the grave too. But he was ill. I no longer know why I would have been afraid of that in particular. Perhaps I didn't want my Liselotte's last journey marred by the presence of a stranger. Maybe I was afraid he would get up with a forty-one-degree fever and really die in the end. But he didn't die, thank God, he got better soon, or almost better. Then he left. Someone came for him. A man appeared suddenly, also from the C-camp, an older man. He went to the parsonage asking about young Kranz and then he came to my house. I wouldn't recognize him. Young Kranz talked to him for a while, then they both left. Probably Richard Kranz thanked me first for the hospitality, but I can't remember his words. There are hours and entire days that are totally lost to me. I was as if in a fog. It happened several times that I got up in the morning, quietly so as not to waken Liselotte. Noiselessly I would walk around the house, would make tea, would put two cups on the table and wait. I waited for a long time. Then I would go into the salon to waken Liselotte. She was not in her bed. Only then did I remember that she was dead.

So right after lunch she went to the woods to get firewood. It was a nice day. You couldn't keep her home anyway when the weather was nice. She got around a lot other days too. She really muffled herself up, put on two or three kerchiefs and off she went. Maybe I shouldn't have let her go. But I didn't want to leave her alone with young Kranz. He was very ill, so nothing would have happened, and I could stake my life on Liselotte anytime. Anyway, she was only fifteen. Still, it wouldn't have been proper. While I wasn't particularly thinking about that gossip business that had poisoned my wife's existence, I certainly knew all about gossip. And this young man that Liselotte would have been left alone with, he wasn't just anybody, but young Kranz of all people. Everyone was already surprised that I, of all people, would take him in. Him of all people. They didn't say so directly to my face, but they whispered. Nobody could prove that young Kranz really did have something to do with my wife who was still the wife of Veit Wallach then. But the opposite was never proven either. At any rate, I could not tolerate it if people were to start gossiping about Liselotte now too. So I let her go. A little later I was in the pharmacy to pick up some medicine for the patient, then I went up to him in the bedroom and stayed at his bedside for a while. I asked him about his plans. He said he didn't have any. He declared, as he had done before, that his whole family had been lost, and I tried to comfort him, since his information was in fact unreliable, somebody's story is, after all, a far cry from proof. And we are dealing here with nothing but stories. There is such a thing as gossip in a C-camp too. And I wanted to encourage him. He was very weak, he couldn't, or wouldn't talk, kept going back to sleep. I waited for Liselotte then, wondering whether her clothes were warm enough. Later on I went out. It started to get dark. I went to meet her. When I didn't find her I turned around. I thought perhaps she was already home.

I wouldn't know any more now which dress she had worn that day, and if I do know it, it is only because I recall every last little detail of the hour that followed, the knock on the door—the doorbell didn't work because there was no electricity then—the people who came into the house, the bottoms of the two shoes, because the soles of her two shoes is what I saw first and only afterwards the blanket they had put her on, at the very last the face. We were used to the weak light of the oil lamp. Still it took a small eternity for me to recognize the face. Nor did I recognize the people right away who had brought Liselotte home. They placed Liselotte on the bed. She was wearing her dark blue coat, blue knee stockings, and the three kerchiefs were still tied around her head. The one on top was brown, it had belonged to her mother. The dress was of a sturdy material, red, flannel, I think. I still have it. I had it cleaned and put it in the closet. The round holes in the back are clearly visible, but the blood is gone, of course. Herr Ambros, the sexton, was there, he kept yelling, or rather groaning, constantly: The Russians, the Russians. It was Ambros who had found the body. The others were silent.

The third reason why I am not in a position to describe the course of events with the necessary precision has to do neither with my emotions nor with my memory. Liselotte left at about two o'clock. She was found at approximately seven o'clock. She lay close to the road. The sexton said that she lay on the right side, with her face on the ground. That is probably right. There was a bit of dirt stuck to the face, that may be why I didn't recognize it right away. Nobody knows what happened in those five hours between two and seven o'clock. The perpetrators were never found. There were men roaming the area in those days, Nazis on the run, C-campers on their way home, foreign workers, deserters, uniformed soldiers, Russian military personnel, tramps, and so forth. There weren't any Russians in our village. But a few days earlier four Russian soldiers had ridden through the village twice, once toward Eichelberg and then back. Frau Mohaupt, the pharmacist's wife, said at the time: The four horsemen of the apocalypse. That is how well-spoken she was. No wonder, with her husband ending up as alderman. Perhaps the four Russians did it, or one of them. At any rate, the shots were fired from a Russian army pistol.

There he lay again, Richard Kranz, not at all sure just where he was lying, in whose house and on whose bed, all was quiet around him in the afternoon light, he saw Jesus Christ in white robe and blue cloak on the moonlit Mount of Olives, the olograph hung above his head, he couldn't see it but he saw it nevertheless, not the painting but the bearded young man with the melancholy eyes, the circle of the halo hovering above his head. To this bearded young man he had once prayed, in the Church of Maria am Gestade, in other churches, and now he no longer knew what he had prayed for and with what words. Nor did he know whether he was lying here still, after that first and second and voluptuous third touch of the cool, soft, clean bedding, or whether he had left the bed after the initial sleep, whether he had gotten up to stroll through Thennberg, to call on Erich Mohaupt's wife in the pharmacy and then on Reverend Horowitz in the parsonage, and then to go to the manor-house and to the manor-house again; the stairs had led to the attic, a spiral staircase without windows, to a brown door behind which were Tante Paula's rooms.

All this was improbable, unreal, a pipe-dream, a nightmare, a single minute of fantasy perhaps, hallucination. What business had he, Richard Kranz, had in a camp, a concentration camp, with total strangers, how had he withstood all that, how had he managed to survive, how had he ended up in a concentration camp within walking distance of Thennberg, the place of summer vacations, holidays, the car had come to a stop in front of the entrance, the bags and suitcases had been stowed away, Richard Kranz had stood in the arch of the entry-way, the cool air held a hint of cat excrement, he had looked at the dusty asphalt, he had worn a white suit of raw silk with big mother-of-pearl buttons, white knee-stockings, white shoes, a round white linen hat on his head, they had driven off, there had been a fairy-tale forest after Hietzing or St. Veit, deer ran across the clearings behind the trees of the Lainz Zoo, but one could never see them clearly, even the Lainz Zoo was already Thennberg, meadows and villages, brooks and bridges, trees and kilometer markers, they all had belonged to Thennberg, the meadows always green and yellow, the villages always bright, dusty and deserted, the brooks always narrow, little rivulets, the bridges always much too long across little water and lots of pebbles, debris and shrubbery, the trees full of fat, juicy leaves, the kilometer markers always painted white, yellowish in the sunlight, and then at some point they had arrived in front of the manor house under the plane trees, summer had started at the Lainz Zoo, and waking up for the first time in the manor house was middle of summer; and how was it that just this one summer close to the concentration camp had stayed, had been preserved, a jar of peach preserves that somebody had left behind, you could open the jar, the peaches hadn't lost their aroma, not their flavor either, there they were, bobbing in the syrup, fish in an aquarium, bright bodies in the dusky grayish green of the shade, Helen Wallach's body, then another body, a girl, Lilo, she lay there, in Aunt Paula's bed, bright, slender, whitish-blonde, her eyes blinking, how was it that it wasn't another one, that it was she of all people—this was all too reasonable, or all too unreasonable, much too beautiful to be true, or much too awful, perhaps all this hadn't really happened, perhaps it was just a hallucination, the real Richard Kranz was a little boy, not yet fourteen, a precocious boy, he lay in his bed in the nursery, in the Brunerstrasse house, he didn't want to go to school, dreaming so he wouldn't have to get up, dreaming a short dream, or maybe that was somebody else's dream: Somewhere, on some night, somebody lay dreaming he was Richard Kranz, summer child in Thennberg, first a Christian, then a Jew, C-camper, he had survived concentration camp, had become a Christian once more, had strolled into the Thennberg summer, returned to the manor house, found sacred Helen again in the form of her moderately sacred daughter Lilo—who could have such a dream, perhaps it was Uncle Edi, boozer, self-anointed squire, ruler over the domains south of the Rivers Drau and Save on behalf of Anglo-Danubia.

No, Eduard Kranz's dream would have been different, more robust, more solid, more vulgar, and above all with a different punch line. If it had been Uncle Edi's dream, Helen would have been still alive, a faded Helen, swinging back and forth between melancholy of old age and lust for life, Helen would not have a husband (Wallach would have been killed in the dream too), but a lover, a young railway man, who nightly stood before her door in full uniform, like a tree in his long overcoat, knocking amorously, faithfully, as a tree-branch knocks against the window pane in the breeze, he would enter and then, in Uncle Edi's dream, the railway man and Helen and, of course, Eduard Kranz (who had just dropped by for one or ten little sips of freshly distilled fruit schnapps) would have a good time with schnapps, bread and bacon, the railway man would tell stories, "Let's see now, how did that happen in Attnang," he would have said, or "I don't care who you are, where's your ticket," and Helen would have laughed, and finally Uncle Edi would have wished the two good luck and bade them good night, he would have said he had to get some fresh air, best go for a little walk with Lilo, with Lilo, for she had been sitting there too, wild, tense, wrapped in her childness, and later, on that walk, between the pigsty and the pigeon-loft, as they were looking at the stars, it had happened: The first kisses and a young maiden's breast gliding tremulously into a man's firmly stroking hand. Richard Kranz lay there, fevered, freezing, burning, he no longer saw Uncle Edi's dream but suddenly he heard his voice. "Between the pigsty and the pigeon-loft," Uncle Edi said—when was that, in which one of the Thennberg summers—? "as we were looking at the stars, and then into the straw." You know, Baron, straw isn't good for a lady's skin, but it's better than hay. "Next morning, when we said good-bye," Uncle Edi's voice said, "she was standing between the vegetable garden and the outhouse, "she looked like a sated cow with her good-natured, veiled eyes." Uncle Edi laughed, Richard Kranz heard no more, suddenly he saw himself.

He was standing in the kitchen, ready to go out, and Lilo was putting the kerchiefs around her head. But what will your father say, Miss Lilo, he, Richard Kranz, had said, and what will you tell your father when he asks you where you've been all this time, Thennberg is so small, much too small, you could say with Frau Mohaupt, or with your girlfriend, or with Reverend Horowitz, so what will you tell him? But as he asked, he had the feeling that someone else was asking these questions through his mouth, you don't ask questions like that of a young girl you love, she'll come up with an answer, cunning and impertinent, one hadn't been given the role of questioner in this piece but the role of hero, and heroes aren't supposed to ask questions, they're supposed to act; hero, big deal, so what does that mean, being a hero, the SS-man Strobl thought of himself as a hero too, and the young Russian who'd shot Adalbert Friedländer, he was a hero too; being a hero wasn't the point at all but being able, finally, to ask, yes, to ask. Obedience smelled of sweat-soaked foot-rags, of empty stomachs with fumes of gastric fluid rising up through toothless mouths, it smelled of festering wounds, of latrines full to overflowing, of cold metal, of rot. But asking smelled like a cake full of raisins on the birthday table, like red tapestry hangings, like needlepoint-covered lounge chairs, like pastel-colored wallpaper in a good restaurant, it smelled like Vienna, hometown, the innermost center of the city after Christmas, when all the many rushing people are gone and a lightly perfumed lady in her lightweight fur coat steps out of the confectioner's shop Demel into Kohlmarkt and stands there for a moment, enveloped in the aroma of cake and coffee, as if helpless, a small parcel dangling from a gloved little finger. To be permitted to ask, that was plain luxury. Lilo knew nothing of all that, nothing of obedience in a C-camp, nothing of the lounge furniture in the Hotel Sacher, she tied her kerchiefs under her chin and, already out on the street, she says: You just leave that up to me, I can wrap Heinz around my little finger, and by the way, what's with that 'Miss Lilo' all of a sudden? Since when are we formal with each other? Come, Richard Kranz said, and then in English, forget it, and she looked at him as if she wanted to spear him on her pointed nose and devour him between her thin, tight lips and her delicately pointed teeth, and as she kept looking at him, he again had the feeling that another was speaking through his mouth, this forget it from the English lessons back home, go to the window, and he would march to the window, where is the window and he would point to it, Italia peninsula est, that was in the Latin class, in the very first freshman Latin class in prep school, where did all that go, and why was it coming back, and why just now? Lilo said: We're having potatoes tonight. He asked: What about it? She said: Because when we have potatoes Heinz doesn't ask anything at all, he just stuffs his belly and leaves me alone. He nodded and enjoyed her voice, and he knew why he wanted to speak English and Latin and talk about his parents, about Erich Mohaupt, about their walks together around the Stephansdom (they had walked around the cathedral under a light snow ten or forty times, discussing poetry and the future of mankind, and Friedrich Nietzsche, Stefan George, Ernst Jünger, and the bitter fate of the poverty-stricken, the unfairness of this world, and much more, and as they told each other their thoughts they also were intent on spitting every ten steps, and the spit had to land on the other one's shoe), and why he wanted to tell about the smell of obedience and about the stench of dying and about the aroma of a good restaurant; he simply wanted to tell her everything. And he said nothing. Perhaps he was running a fever. Then they were under the plane trees and had entered the manor house through the open door, and now he really wanted to start talking. He spoke, and again had the feeling of a strange voice speaking through his mouth.

Did you see the rocking-chair before, he asked, my uncle always used to sit in that chair, his name was Eduard Kranz and he was in the insurance business. Finished, period. Lilo didn't even raise her eyes, why should she, anyone can have an uncle who sits in a rocking-chair, and everybody's uncle could be in the insurance business. My uncle is a gardener in Schrunz, Lilo said, my father's brother, but I've never seen him. A crate filled with wadded-up newspaper stood in the living room, but Aunt Paula's Chinese vase wasn't there, so there was nothing to be said about Aunt Paula, nothing about her singing school in Zurich and nothing about the Italian singer who could be seen in the brooch below her wrinkled neck with his mouth wide open in the role of Rigoletto. The wood paneling in the former den was practically undamaged. The room before, said Richard Kranz, that was the living room, the rocking chair used to stand in the living room. And then, in the bedroom, he said: Here was my mother's bed. Lilo asked: And where did your father sleep? They used to tell that it was a bed from the time of Louis the Fourteenth, said Richard Kranz. And your father? asked Lilo. He wasn't here often, Richard Kranz said, and when he was he slept in the den. And he should have told about everything, Uncle Edi's loud voice under the window, Aunt Paula's fate, Jakob Rombach's life and Grandmother Kranz's battle for Christian salvation, Father's frequent flights to somewhere, some spa, the precipitous departures to Abbazia, the blooming of the shrubs behind the music pavilion erupting in lunacy, the hysterical blue blaze in the eyes of Agnes Deutsch, but all he said was: You look like a girl I used to know. In Vienna? Lilo asked. He said: No, in Abbazia. A nice girl? Lilo asked, her nose pointedly inquisitive, by then they stood in the hall before the windowless spiral staircase, what could he say, he said: Yes, sure. She asked: Was she very nice? And then she said: It's cold here, and Richard Kranz said: It's warmer upstairs. He was freezing, maybe he was running a fever.

It was really warmer behind the brown door in Aunt Paula's rooms, the sun beat down on the roof, the rooms were small, everything was in its place, in front of the mirror, a few reddish-brown, maybe silvery, hairs glistened between the teeth of the comb. Lilo scampered out into the bathroom, smelled at the egg-shaped cake of soap, flew through the living room into the bedroom and to the night table, looked at the book, *Ulrike Woytich* by Jakob Wassermann, ran to the window, looked out, hopped about like a canary in a cage, she had pulled the first kerchief from her head and then the second and the third, had slipped out of her coat, she was wearing a red dress of sturdy material, it could have been flannel, and finally she had asked: Did the girl live here? Richard Kranz said nothing. Was she nicer then me? Lilo asked. Leave her be, said Richard Kranz, she is undoubtedly no longer alive, he wanted to say, they burned her, even her blue hysterical stare got burned someplace, such a thing goes real quick, takes no time to turn two jellied marbles in two eye sockets into a few grains of dust. He did not say it but took Lilo's hand in his and raised it up, studying the fingers one after the other, studying them thoroughly, young-girl fingers, not altogether clean, the knuckles slightly red, the cuticle around the thumb ragged, nails cut off straight across, too short, he looked at them and kissed the too-red fingertips, one after the other; thin young-girl fingers burn fast, he wanted to say but he didn't say it, then he kissed the narrow mouth, the lips were chapped, impatient, clumsy; thin young-girl lips burn fast, he thought, silently, kissed the narrow mouth, between the two rows of teeth, delicate and sharp, he found the young-girl tongue, pointed, agile, even all-too-lively tongues are quickly turned into a few grains of dust, he wanted to say but didn't say, didn't want to think any longer; the red flannel dress had a zipper at the left side of the waist, it made a whirring sound.

Richard Kranz opened his eyes. He hadn't seen a woman in five years, he'd never seen a woman half undressed like this, in a white slip that was no longer quite white, in a pink camisole that reached almost down to the knees. Come, he said, and again another spoke through his mouth, there aren't any drapes or shades here, and as he was saying this he thought: Why am I forever apologizing? And at the same moment he asked himself why he had said that, and to whom and in whose voice.

He took off his coat, slipped out of his shirt and pants, the last time he had taken off his clothes in broad daylight it had been for the delousing, and afterwards they had walked across to the showers. There was talk about how there were camps where gas came out of the shower heads instead of water, or how they had to get undressed to get shot, naked bodies huddling together, naked mountains of human flesh collapsing somewhere, burning up, rotting. Richard Kranz said: I love you. He held on to that sentence, pulled himself back to the manor house, to Aunt Paula's rooms, back into his childhood that had disappeared, back—but to where? For a second he looked at himself as if for the last time, at that emaciated body of a grown man, it was foreign, where had that boy disappeared to, that boy from the house in Brunerstrasse, a strange man was standing here in broad day-light, a piece of livestock, naked, as though ready to die: he pushed forward with his gaunt hips, following the rigid muscle-chord of his penis, this member that was pulling his body along behind it, he had never seen it either, who was this man who between the chilly surfaces of sheet and coverlet was pressing against a warm body, the body of a woman, he must look at her.

The whitish-blonde hair covered her face, only the nose was sticking out, and the pale, narrow lips revealed the delicate, sharp teeth, the mouth was smiling, the neck long, shoulders angular, a hint of hair at the armpits, the chest reminiscent of a narrow coffin with something still alive in it, the sex was like the smiling mouth of a very young girl.

You are beautiful, said Richard Kranz, to her and even more so that he could believe it, yes, beautiful, young, strange, she had taken her clothes off without asking any questions, she lay there waiting, opening her eyes for a moment, closing them again. God, is it cold here, she said, and Richard Kranz suddenly heard Uncle Edi's voice, "Between the pigsty and the pigeon-loft, as we looked at the stars, and then into the straw," and then Phoebus Silberman asked what the breasts had de facto looked like, and Aunt Paula walked around, in the morning she always wore a silk scarf around her wrinkled neck. Then they disappeared, Uncle Edi, Phoebus Silberman, Aunt Paula; the girl said something, Richard Kranz didn't get it, he was freezing, surely he was running a fever. The body against which he snuggled was smooth and warm, Richard Kranz closed his eyes so he could see himself, see the lovers in Aunt Paula's bed; the picture appeared on the inside of his forehead, a pretty sight, but Lilo moved and again said something, the picture disappeared, and suddenly he was overcome with the feeling that he had to take off his own body and then take more off the girl too, peel her away from her body in order to cleanse her from the rot in her vagina—he held Lilo in his arms but she was separated from him by layers upon layers of naked flesh that was doomed to death, that was hidden under her skin which would dissolve, that was protected by all-too delicate ribs, beyond reach. I love you, he murmured into her ear, whispered into her mouth, I love you. His penis lay against her thigh, snail-soft, languid, moistened from her vagina, touching the sparse silky hair of her pubis.

Perhaps he hadn't said anything, perhaps he hadn't lain with her in Aunt Paula's bed at all, perhaps he only dreamed that Lilo had stood in front of the tall mirror that was mounted into the door of the wardrobe, stark naked in the cold, her abdomen curved out, her tiny breasts pointed up stiffly, that she had studied herself in the mirror and then said: So, we put our clothes back on now. Perhaps they hadn't left the manor house later, and walked silently through some village in the dusk, perhaps it wasn't Thennberg at all. The clouds look like whipped cream, he had said, can you get whipped cream for coffee again? She said: But there aren't any clouds. He was running a fever.

What did she say? asked Heinrich Moravec. He was sitting on the edge of the bed smoking a cigarette and looking at him, the sick one whose name was Richard Kranz. The name was like a label on a bottle, important, unimportant, the final testimony of his parents' carnal pleasure, shape of their lust. Did I really tell everything to Moravec? thought Richard Kranz. So, said Heinrich Moravec, at the manor-house. Richard Kranz nodded. We will go away, Lilo and I, he said later, opening his eyes and looking into Heinrich Moravec's eyes, he wanted to sit up but he fell back into the pillows, and he saw the angular shoulders and the smiling young-girl lips amid the whitish-blonde silky bush of hair and the delicate, pointed teeth between the chapped lips, and still Heinrich Moravec was sitting on the edge of the bed, still smoking his cigarette, and then asking: What exactly are your plans? Richard Kranz said: My parents are dead, I know, my uncle is dead too, maybe my Aunt in Zurich is alive, but she won't be alive much longer, so what are my plans, I'll make it, someplace, we'll make it. You mean you and Lilo? asked Heinrich Moravec. Richard Kranz nodded a second time. He was looking into hard eyes.

Then they disappeared too, the eyes of Heinrich Moravec, and Jesus Christ sat on the Mount of Olives in his white robe and blue cloak by the light of the moon, a bearded man, melancholy, he looked like Markus Löw. And later Richard Kranz no longer knew in whose house he lay and in whose bed, there was silence around him, afternoon light, and he had the feeling that the marrow in his spine had turned to ice, and his eyes were frozen and were pressing against the taut skin of his lids. Whose eyes are they, the eyes of some strange man, thought Richard Kranz, it is a strange pain in a stranger's eyes. And then, much later, someone knocked on the door downstairs, chairs were being pushed aside, many people speaking at the same time, and a man's hoarse voice kept repeating: The Russians, the Russians.

The Russians, said Richard Kranz, everybody says the Russians killed her, but I tell you that's not right. He was standing in front of the window in Heinrich Moravec's bedroom, dressed, on shaky legs, bent, almost reeling, and opposite him, in front of the door, where a few days ago Jesus Christ had floated in white robe and blue cloak, there now stood a man, dark, bearded, melancholy, Markus Löw.

What are you talking about? asked Markus Löw, it sounded soft and squeaky, as if each word were a rusty pail being pulled by a rusty chain out of a dirty well. What kind of talk is that? asked Markus Löw. How can you say to me, "I tell you," when it is clear that you are doing the telling and not I, don't tell me that you're proud your mother taught you how to speak, and what do you mean by "everybody says?" If everybody says it then nobody says it. And how can you say, "that's not right?" How come you know what's right? I know it, Richard Kranz said, he was freezing, maybe he was running a fever still. No, I'm not proud, he said, but I know who it was. So what if you know, asked Markus Löw. What if you know better than all the others? Number one: why should you know better? and number two: who'll believe that you know better? Richard Kranz said nothing for a while, because he wanted to say two things at the same time, twenty things at the same time, they thrust themselves up, pushed together in his head, wanting to be put into words, and finally he said: I will prove it.

You will prove something? asked Markus Löw in a soft and squeaky voice. You of all people will prove something, when you should be glad that they didn't beat you to death or shoot you, as they shot this girl so as not to shoot you, you who came along without anybody asking you, just because some Director Kranz and his family once lived here, and who asked Director Kranz to come here? In order to prove something you need three things: You need one who wants to prove something, you need another one who listens to him, and you need something that should be proved. So now we have one who wants to prove something, but that's all, because nobody wants to listen to him and the thing he wants to prove is long over with, the victim is in the ground and the murderer is running around somewhere. Is he the only murderer running around? A thousand murderers are running around, ten thousand murderers, and one will get locked up and the next one will keep running around and God will punish him or he won't. Do you want to play God or something, asked Markus Löw? And will the girl come back to life if you play God?

She went out, said Richard Kranz, I don't know just when that was, I was lying here, I had a fever, I'm sure he sent her away, somehow, under some pretext, he sent her into the woods and then he went after her and shot her. She was shot with a Russian pistol, but why couldn't he have had a Russian pistol, there are pistols lying around everywhere, German ones and Russian ones, it isn't difficult to have a Russian pistol. And then he came back and sat down with me again, and then they brought the body, and so who could have done it, of course the Russians.

Had he been with you before, asked Markus Löw? Richard Kranz said nothing at first, then he nodded, and when Markus Löw asked once more he said: Yes, he was here before, and I told him everything.

You have to tell everything all the time, don't you, said Markus Löw. You want to say everything all the time and prove everything all the time, because you pride yourself that you can say everything and prove everything, you don't know just when he was with you the first time and just when she went out you don't know either, but you want to prove everything. And because you are so proud and because you know everything better than anybody else and you have to tell everybody, others must die. He sure didn't kill her because he wanted to kill her, he killed her because he didn't want her to be with you, because he didn't want her to leave him, she was his only child, and suddenly the only child wants to run away, and not with just anybody but with a Jew. Richard Kranz said: I'm not a Jew. Markus Löw seemed not to hear it. He couldn't touch the Jew, of course, he said, no, not him, he just came out of C-camp, there would have been complications, because why would the Russians be shooting a Jew who just came out of C-camp? And so, with a heavy heart, he had to make the decision rather to kill his own child, because why wouldn't the Russians kill a young girl? Maybe they wanted to rape the girl, maybe the girl screamed, maybe someone was coming just then, maybe they shot the girl quickly. And now you come along, you who always knows everything better, and you want to prove everything? You want to prove that you turned the girl's head so she wanted to run away with you, and so now you want to prove that you practically badgered the father, dear father, hurry up and kill her, that you put the pistol in his hand, that you drove him to shoot her?

I didn't know, said Richard Kranz.

Why didn't you know that, of all things, asked Markus Löw? You know everything else. The only thing you don't know is when you told him to kill her and when she left and when she was shot and when they found her and when they brought her back, and another thing you don't know is how people are, otherwise you know everything. Go run to the police and say, Mister Policeman, My name is so and so, and over there someplace a girl got shot with a Russian pistol, but so and so did it, not the Russians but her father, I demand that you take her out of her grave and kill her father instead, for there must be justice.

There must be justice, said Richard Kranz. He swayed and had to sit down, and he looked into the face of the dark, bearded, melancholy man who was smiling now, pensively and kindly, it was the face of the Jesus Christ of the olograph, and the voice was no longer squeaky, it was even softer now, a merry, tinkling, happy whisper.

Why? the merry, tinkling whisper-voice asked, and Markus Löw was still smiling, he had no teeth, his bearded lips widened, it was the toothless mouth of a smiling infant. Why must there be justice, the voice asked? You see, my son, that is precisely the great mistake, for who says that there must be justice? And who has the right to decide what is justice? Let us assume the father really did shoot his daughter. But what kind of father? A cripple. A cripple needs his child in order to live, he needs her like he needs his cane, in order to walk. Is it justice to take his only hope from a limping cripple? Just because young Mr. Kranz suddenly comes along and says: This and this is mine from now on? Is it justice to say to the father: You must give her up. And even if he is only a stepfather, does he not have the right to say: No, I will not give her up, I'd rather have her lie under the ground than under you? All right, you can answer, all right, but is it justice to destroy the happiness of two young people? Let's say they found each other and now they want to run away. Is it justice to keep them from going? But if you say that, my son, then I can ask: Is it justice to give a young girl such a choice: Either you stay with your father or you come with me? How should she decide? If she stays with the father she has possibly wrecked her life, if she leaves her father she has wrecked his life, and she may have wrecked her own life in the bargain as well, because how long does such a love last anyway? It can last fifty years and it can last five days, who can tell in advance? And isn't it better for the girl to stay here where she was born? Who has the right to take her from her village and carry her into the world? You of all people have the right? Why you? Just because you love her? But whom do you really love, do you really love the girl or do you only love yourself? And if you are permitted to love yourself, is not the father also permitted to love himself? You want justice? Markus Löw smiled again, and the voice sounded still softer and merrier. I'll tell you a secret, said the voice, there is no such thing as justice.

But there is such a thing as love, said Richard Kranz.

If you know everything better, the voice said ever softer and ever merrier, then you could keel over dead on the spot, you could have died for the girl, because anyone who has nothing more to learn, what's the point of staying alive at all? But you do not really know everything better, you know absolutely nothing, you came here to the village where you used to be as a little boy, a refined child, now you are no longer a refined child but somebody who comes along and lets himself be put up in a house that isn't his house, and gets involved with a girl who is not there for his benefit, and right away the girl has to die, only because you don't know how people are and how life is, because first you were a spoiled child and then you were in C-camp, and all the time they made sure that you'd never find out what other people are like and what you are like, and what havoc you could create when you do right and when you do wrong. You don't know what you are doing, nobody knows what they're doing, one does something evil and good comes out of it, another does something good and evil comes out of it. And since this is so, we shouldn't interfere, why do you have to interfere? If you want to remain a decent human being you shouldn't live your life whole but only half, so only one half will get dirty and the other half will stay clean. I'll tell you another secret, the voice said, barely audible and so merry that it seemed to be about to tell a joke but the punch line is so good, so very good, that all that premature merriment laughs it into the ground. One should live, snorted the voice softly, as if one were already dead. What's the point of living then? asked Richard Kranz.

How should I know? the voice answered. Who needs to think about that? God wanted it so.

But why? asked Richard Kranz.

Do you by any chance want to know what God thought about it, whispered the voice? If he thinks, he won't tell, and if he doesn't think he can't tell either. Leave the good Lord alone, I came by to pick you up, so now don't hold us up any longer.

Richard Kranz wanted to say that he didn't want to go before he—before what? And words like murder and love turned into a single motion: he raised his shoulders a little and opened his arms, the two palms hanging in mid-air, stiff, open, helpless.

Are you Saint George, asked and answered the voice, it was the voice of Markus Löw once more. You can love her tomorrow and day-after-tomorrow, he squeaked softly, and why are you so upset, just because she got killed? Many got killed, and nobody will breathe life into them again, and nobody will revenge them and all of them will be forgotten. Don't upset yourself, if God isn't upset, so he said thou shalt not kill, and when people kill, what does he do? Nothing, that's what. Come.

I'm not a Jew, said Richard Kranz, and perhaps another was speaking through his mouth again, he wasn't sure, I am not a Jew, I believe in everlasting life and that a murderer goes to Hell and Lilo to Heaven, I will see her again, it can't be that I will never see her again.

And if you see her again? asked Markus Löw. And if the murderer really does go to Hell? What good'll it do you? Come, don't hold us up any longer, pack your things.

I don't have any things, said Richard Kranz. He followed behind Markus Löw, walked into the kitchen and saw Heinrich Moravec seated at the table, automatically, as if in a dream, he shook his hand, thanked him, he didn't want to shake his hand and didn't want to say anything but both of these things had now taken place, what kind of man am I, he though wretchedly, to—with a murderer—but he had already left the house and saw Markus Löw standing in front of the entrance, smilingly admiring the antlers of the royal stag. Come, said Markus Löw, turning, and Richard Kranz followed behind, past the pharmacy and the church, past the cemetery, past the manor house he walked slowly and heavily, the muddy yellow surface of a puddle puckered under his foot, the water rose, subsided again, clods of mud stuck to the soles, slippery with every step. Where are we going? asked Richard Kranz, he had finally caught up with Markus Löw, and without stopping he said: so where should we go? We go down to the big street and then on to Vienna, and there'll be a stream on the way, any old stream, and there'll be a stone too and a fish as well, come, as long as we can move our legs we keep walking, and you needn't bother asking why.

Afterword

Thennberg occupies an important place in Sebestyén's oeuvre. It is the last—and best of his early novels; after its appearance in 1969 he concentrated on cultural journalism and, although he did continue to write short stories, he did not publish another novel until *A Man too White* in 1984. As well as being the culmination point of his early period, *Thennberg*, with its theme of the search for time past and its narration from differing points of view, anticipates Sebestyén's masterpiece, *The Works of Solitude*, published in 1986.

György Sebestyén was born in 1930 into the comfortable and cultured Hungarian middle class. The family firm of tailors, founded by his grandfather and run by his father and uncle, was patronized by diplomats and the stars of the Budapest stage. As was traditional among the Budapest bourgeoisie, Sebestyén and his stepsister were brought up by German-speaking nannies and governesses, so that he spoke German before he began to express himself in his native Hungarian; these same redoubtable ladies taught them English and French by the same direct method. The legacy for Sebestyén of this multilingual infancy was a special sensitivity to language, "a sharpened feeling for the tone colors of words and the sound patterns of sentences," as he said in an autobiographical sketch.

His early familiarity with several major European languages led to extensive reading and a precocious interest in philosophical, cultural and social questions, as well as in literature. At thirteen he translated (for himself) Rilke's *The Tale of the Love and Death of Cornet Christopher Rilke*, and while still at school he published essays and articles, and edited a volume of recent Hungarian poets.

His development after the Second World War was typical of that of many middle-class, East-European intellectuals. Despite his sheltered upbringing, he had a strong personal response to social injustice, and this, together with his affinity for the Russian Narodniks—populists who went to live with the peasants they supported—and his interest in the work of the Hungarian musicologists and ethnographers who researched village life, all seemed to find legitimate political expression in the Hungarian Communist Party, which he joined soon after the War. He studied at Budapest University, first literature and philosophy, later ethnography—and at the same time worked in the theater and as a journalist, eventually having responsibility for the cultural sections of *Magyar Nemzet* (The Hungarian Nation). Like all newspapers in Hungary at the time, like Sebestyén himself, *Magyar Nemzet* was committed to propagating the Party line. Although there were events such as the Rajk trial in 1949, the disappearance of friends, and the gagging of intellectuals, which puzzled and disturbed him, he for a long time maintained his belief that the Party, which he saw as the physical embodiment of his own youthful enthusiasms, must be right. His growing disillusionment was repressed: for a while it found a safety valve in his involvement in the Petöfi Circle, a discussion group of intellectuals tolerated, if not approved of, by the Party, and on which Sebestyén reported at length in *Magyar Nemzet*; but when the uprising of 1956 came, he found his earlier enthusiasm rekindled, but this time the revolution was directed against the Party. After the uprising had been crushed by Soviet troops, he left Hungary for Vienna in December 1956.

Once he had settled in Austria, it did not take Sebestyén long to realize that he did not want to become an emigré intellectual, writing in a language with which he had lost contact, books that would never be published in the country for which they were intended. He decided to become an Austrian writer. This meant reviving the German of his early years until it was a vehicle for cultural and literary expression. How well he succeeded can be seen from the fact that in 1988, two years before his early death from cancer, he was elected President of the PEN Club of his adopted country, a position he used to help young and unknown writers, thus repaying the assistance he had received thirty years earlier from Franz Theodor Csokor, Erika Hanel, Herbert Eisenreich and other members of the Austrian PEN.

Sebestyén wrote his first novel after his arrival in Vienna. He wrote it in Hungarian and had it translated—by the brother of the Austro-Hungarian dramatist, Ödön von Horváth, revised by Erika Hanel. It took the uprising of 1956 as its subject, and the title—*Die Türen schließen sich*

(*The Doors are Closing* , 1957)—reflected his own sense of being cut off from his past. His second novel, *Der Mann im Sattel* (Man in the Saddle, 1961), he wrote in Hungarian, then set it aside and rewrote it in German himself. He still needed a great deal of help with corrections from his friends, but by the time he wrote his third novel, *Die Schule der Verführung* (The School of Seduction, 1964), his control of German was assured, and already revealed his own distinctive mixture of lyricism combined with acute observation of detail.

Thennberg appeared in 1969, but then there was a gap before his next novel, *Albino (A Man too White)*, appeared in 1984. In the student movement of the late sixties, Sebestyén saw dangerous parallels to the youthful enthusiasms which had led him to accept the authority of the Communist Party, and for more than a decade he abandoned novels for cultural writings—articles and essays, travel books, and, above all, the editorship of *Pannonia,* the "Magazine for European Cooperation." His "resistance to false prophets, to a spiritual regression which puts on a progressive face," was not a direct attack in the political field, but an attempt to build bridges between East and West through cultural contacts at a time when other avenues were blocked. He worked to establish a sense of common central European culture across the Iron Curtain, the disappearance of which was fulfillment which his early death did not allow him fully to enjoy.

The narrative of *Thennberg*, like that of his later large-scale novel, *The Works of Solitude*, is multifaceted: the various chapters are narrated from the perspective and viewpoint of different characters, and the narrative mode varies from third-person narration to first- and third-person interior monologue, to direct speech. Through these separate lenses the story focuses on the figure of Richard Kranz, a young Austrian Jew from a wealthy family that has converted to Catholicism (he repeatedly maintains, "I'm not a Jew.") He has spent the Hitler period in concentration camps and survived: the last camp was near to the Austrian village of Thennberg, where his family used to spend the summer holidays before 1938.

The "attempted return" of the subtitle refers to Kranz' desire to recreate the idyllic past of those summer holidays. This "search for time past" ends in failure, and emphasizes the lesson Sebestyén himself had learned so quickly after he left Hungary: the past is past and trying to resurrect it will lead either to failure or at most to the sterile conservation of something lifeless, like the tinned peaches that are one of the several symbols of this theme. The end is left open, undefined: Kranz disappears, presumably having accepted that the past cannot be recaptured.

Thennberg is only incidentally "Holocaust literature." Although Sebestyén himself had some Jewish ancestry, he does not dwell at all on the horrors of the concentration camps, nor on the anti-Semitism of some of the inhabitants of the village. Kranz's Jewishness is only one, fairly minor, element among others that mean he does not belong; more important is the fact that he comes from outside, from the capital, and from a different social class, his father being a wealthy banker. What Sebestyén does in *Thennberg* is to present the Holocaust as an established fact of central European history. And when the mask slips to reveal the casual, everyday fascism of a character like Moravec, the effect is as disturbing, if not as horrifying, as more detailed depictions.

Although the past cannot be recovered, it can be evoked. The various monologues and musings, statements and confessions, of which the book is made up, coalesce into a picture of a past society—the central European bourgeoisie—that disappeared with the Second World War. This portrait is not extensive in detail, but intensive in the evocation of the atmosphere of the social stratum in which Sebestyén himself grew up. (A similar, but more extended evocation is to be found in *The Works of Solitude*).

But Sebestyén is not only a social novelist who is concerned to recreate past society. He is also a moralist and philosopher who is interested in perennial aspects of human condition. His figures exude an almost lyrical sense of their own individuality combined with a precise placement within the social order, but they also illuminate wider aspects of human nature. One such is the central theme of the sterility of attempts to preserve the past; another is the motif of playing a role of hiding behind a mask; a third is the close relationship between love and death, between *eros* and *thanatos*, which permeates much of Sebestyén's work. It is this depth, which emerges indirectly from the material rather than buttonholing the reader, which makes Sebestyén a worthy heir to the great Austrian tradition of the novel from Robert Musil to Heimito von Doderer.

Michael Mitchell

ARIADNE PRESS
Studies in Austrian Literature, Culture and Thought

*Major Figures of
Modern Austrian Literature*
Edited and Introduced
by Donald G. Daviau

*Major Figures of Turn-of-the-Century
Austrian Literature*
Edited and Introduced
by Donald G. Daviau

*Austrian Writers and the
Anschluss: Understanding the
Past—Overcoming the Past*
Edited and Introduced
by Donald G. Daviau

*Introducing Austria
A Short History*
By Lonnie Johnson

*Coexistent Contradictions
Joseph Roth in Retrospect*
Edited by
Helen Chambers

*The Verbal and Visual Art of
Alfred Kubin*
By Phillip H. Rhein

*Kafka and Language
In the Stream of
Thoughts and Life*
By G. von Natzmer Cooper

*Robert Musil and the Tradition
of the German Novelle*
By Kathleen O'Connor

*Blind Reflections:
Gender in Elias Canetti's*
Die Blendung
By Kristie A. Foell

Conversations with Peter Rosei
By Wilhelm Schwarz

*Austria in the Thirties
Culture and Politics*
Edited by Kenneth Segar
and John Warren

*Stefan Zweig:
An International Bibliography*
By Randolph J. Klawiter

*Austrian Foreign Policy
Yearbook*
Report of the Austrian Federal
Ministry for Foreign Affairs
for the Year 1990

*Quietude and Quest
Protagonists and Antagonists in
the Theater, on and off Stage
As Seen Through the Eyes of
Leon Askin*
Leon Askin and C. Melvin Davidson

*"What People Call Pessimism":
Sigmund Freud, Arthur Schnitzler
and Nineteenth-Century
Controversy at the University
of Vienna Medical School*
By Mark Luprecht

Arthur Schnitzler and Politics
By Adrian Clive Roberts

*Structures of Disintegration
Narrative Strategies in
Elias Canetti's* Die Blendung
By David Darby

*Of Reason and Love
The Life and Work of Marie von
Ebner-Eschenbach*
By Carl Steiner

*Franz Kafka:
A Writers Life*
By Joachim Unseld

ARIADNE PRESS
Translation Series:

February Shadows
By Elisabeth Reichart
Translated by Donna L. Hoffmeister
Afterword by Christa Wolf

Night Over Vienna
By Lili Körber
Translation by Viktoria Hertling
& Kay M. Stone. Commentary by
Viktoria Hertling

The Cool Million
By Erich Wolfgang Skwara
Translated by Harvey I. Dunkle
Preface by Martin Walser
Afterword by Richard Exner

Buried in the Sands of Time
Poetry by Janko Ferk
English/German/Slovenian
English Translation by H. Kuhner

Puntigam or The Art of Forgetting
By Gerald Szyszkowitz
Translated by Adrian Del Caro
Preface by Simon Wiesenthal
Afterword by Jürgen Koppensteiner

Negatives of My Father
By Peter Henisch
Translation and Afterword
by Anne C. Ulmer

On the Other Side
By Gerald Szyszkowitz
Translated by Todd C. Hanlin
Afterword by Jürgen Koppensteiner

The Slackers and Other Plays
By Peter Turrini
Translation and Afterword
by Richard S. Dixon

The Baron and the Fish
By Peter Marginter
Translation and Afterword
by Lowell A. Bangerter

*I Want to Speak
The Tragedy and Banality
of Survival in
Terezin and Auschwitz*
By Margareta Glas-Larsson
Edited and with a Commentary
by Gerhard Botz
Translated by Lowell A. Bangerter

The Works of Solitude
By György Sebestyén
Translation and Afterword
by Michael Mitchell

Krystyna
By Simon Wiesenthal
Translated by Eva Dukes

Deserter
By Anton Fuchs
Translation and Afterword
by Todd C. Hanlin

From Here to There
By Peter Rosei
Translation and Afterword
by Kathleen Thorpe

The Angel of the West Window
By Gustav Meyrink
Translated by Michael Mitchell

*Relationships
An Anthology of Contemporary
Austrian Literature*
Selected and with an Introduction
by Adolf Opel

Three Late Plays
By Arthur Schnitzler
Translation and Afterword
G.J. Weinberger

Professor Bernhardi and Other Plays
By Arthur Schnitzler
Translation G.J. Weinberger
Afterword Jeffrey B. Berlin

Translations Series:

The Bengal Tiger
By Jeannie Ebner
Translation and Afterword
by Lowell A. Bangerter

Three Flute Notes
By Jeannie Ebner
Translation and Afterword
by Lowell A. Bangerter

Farewell to Love and Other Misunderstandings
By Herbert Eisenreich
Translation and Afterword
by Renate Latimer

The Sphere of Glass
By Marianne Gruber
Translation and Afterword
by Alexandra Strelka
Preface by Joseph P. Strelka

A Man Too White
By György Sebestén
Translation and Afterword
by Michael Mitchell

The Green Face
By Gustav Meyrink
Translated by Michael Mitchell

*The Ariadne Book of Austrian Fantasy
The Meyrink Years 1890-1930*
Edited and translated
by Michael Mitchell

Walpurgisnacht
By Gustav Meyrink
Translated by Michael Mitchell

On the Wrong Track
By Milo Dor
Translated by Jerry Glenn
and Jennifer Kelley

Night Train
By Friederike Mayröcker
Translation and Afterword
by Beth Bjorklund

Memories With Trees
By Ilse Tielsch
Translation and Afterword
by David Scrase

Return to the Center
By Otto von Habsburg
Translated by Carvel de Bussy

View from a Distance
By Lore Lizbeth Waller

Five Plays
By Gerald Szyszkowitz
Translated by Todd Hanlin, Heidi Hutchinson and Joseph McVeigh

Anthology of Contemporary Austrian Folk Plays
By Veza Canetti, Peter Preses & Ulrich Becher, Felix Mitterer, Gerald Szyszkowitz, Peter Turrini
Translation and Afterword
by Richard Dixon

The Condemned Judge
By Janko Ferk
Translation and Afterword
by Lowell A. Bangerter

Thomas Bernhard and His Grandfather: "Our Grandfathers Are Our Teachers."
By Caroline Markolin
Translated by Petra Hartweg

The Convent School
By Barbara Frischmuth
Translated by
Gerald Chapple and James B. Lawson

The Calm Ocean
By Gerhard Roth
Translated by Helga Schreckenberger
and Jacqueline Vansant

Remembering Gardens
by Kurt Klinger
Translated by Harvey I. Dunkle